D'ANDRE WALKER

Not Only in Blood

To my family.

"He had lived and acted on the assumption that he was alone, and now he saw that he had not been. What he had done made others suffer. No matter how much he would long for them to forget him, they would not be able to. His family was a part of him, not only in blood, but in spirit."

Richard Wright, *Native Son*

1

The Boy

Two sturdily built horses pulled a small wooden carriage over an old, worn trail. The so-called Indians had traversed down the tree-lined path for hundreds of years. The roaring of the wheels drowned out the pit pat of the hooves as they continued to wear away at the dirt. No more than one foot of separation sat between a boy and a man who rode together at the front. A quick study of the two revealed that they were, without a doubt, father and son. The tall duo looked to be uncomfortable, with their knees sitting up high and tight. Despite his youthful age, the boy was already long and lank. When he walked, his arms swung wildly, making him appear goofy and awkward. Behind them, packed in cages, were several chickens on their way to the market. At each bump, the chickens erupted into a deafening frenzy. The boy looked over at his father and yelled to make himself audible.

"I don't know, Paw. I think I could've whooped you."

"I had been workin' day in and day out since I was prob'ly five years old. By the time I was your age, I could wrastle a steer down to the ground, no problem."

"I'm smarter than a steer."

"Not by much."

They both laughed from deep in their stomachs.

"You thin and quick," said the father in a voice strong enough to rattle loose rocks. "But all I need to do is get my hands on you. You won't get away." He dropped the reins and simulated himself grabbing a hold of the boy.

"You might be stronger, but my arms are longer. You wouldn't touch me 'cause I'd just keep you back, and besides, you was always tired from 'workin' them fields,' you'd be an easy win."

"I was strong as an ox and could toss a millstone clear across the Mississippi!"

They continued to joke and took no notice of the colossal cotton plantations they passed. The ominous yet beautiful homes sat a quarter of a mile back from the main road. Coming closer to the small settlement of Memphis, they passed run-down-looking homes that paled in comparison to the mighty plantations.

When they entered Memphis, both knew to wipe the smiles off their identical faces. The father's face sat hardened by a life of labor, anger, and torment. The son had been sheltered from the harsh realities of his father's world. Bright brown eyes beheld his untouched innocence. The two lived in a country that held those who looked like them in physical and mental shackles. Because of this, the father had vowed that his children would be born free and never endure the many hardships he had.

In the town, they passed a building made of rotting wood. Painted on this building in big white letters were the words GENERAL STORE. An old white man sat calmly in an even older chair outside of it. Dressed in overalls and dark-brown jackboots, he tilted his chair back and forth. He removed the pipe from his mouth and glared at the two with a look of disapproval. When the boy returned a stare, his father tilted his hat to the man, who replied by spitting off to the side of him.

"We gone over this many times now. You gotta watch where you starin,'" the father scolded. The boy sat with a dumbfounded look on his face but said nothing.

The city had been founded six years prior. Despite its run-down appearance, it hummed loud with commerce. The two came to an open-air market where they were surrounded with merchants like themselves. The boy was often forced to stand alone with the chickens and tobacco, a task he hated. From afar, he watched his father whisper with several men, some white, some black. He never heard the conversations, but their facial expressions suggested seriousness.

Often the boy sat idle and would half watch the town's processions, his mind being far away. Black men drove by in beautiful horse-drawn carriages with white occupants in them. This always caught his attention above all else. He sat frustrated at not being able to form a respectable critique of the uneasiness it caused him. After he sold off all the merchandise, they headed back east, opposite the way of the retreating sun.

"I don't know how many times I have to tell you," said the father, still angry from earlier. "Don't go all reckless staring them down like that."

"But why? He was lookin' at me. I ain't do nothing wrong but look back."

"I know, son, but that's the way things are."

"You always say to follow the Bible. Well, God ain't never said we can't look a white man in the eye."

"Son, I agree with you. All I say is, if you open that pot, you gonna have to eat what's in it."

The boy didn't have time to question this riddle. Two dark figures on horseback appeared several hundred yards in front of them. The tunnel of trees and branches turned the two riders into sinister silhouettes. They trotted along with their heads facing off to the sides of the trail, peering into the endless trees.

They came closer and, with a menacing face, one of the two men locked eyes with the boy. He pulled his wild-looking horse in front of their carriage, and his partner followed suit. The boy's father yanked back on the reins, causing the horses to scream in anguish. The two parties entered a standoff as the horses of the two men began to chomp and snarl like ferocious dogs. One of the men sat with his hand on his pistol and watched the two of them with hawk eyes. His hat hid the majority of his mustached face, which was a dark-pink color due to years of abuse from the sun. The boy's body paralyzed and tensed up, his pulsing heart, the only moving thing in him. His father now sat with his right hand on his thigh. In reaching distance, a few inches below, was a pistol in a bag on the floor of the carriage.

"C'mon. You know how this works. Let me see your passes, boy," the man said to the father. The other man spat tobacco and took his horse to the back of the carriage. He began to push around the empty cages and knocked on the wood as if he were looking for something.

The boy and his father took out small metal tins that contained their freedom papers. The boy handed his to his father, who showed them to the man. He looked at the father's and read aloud.

"State of Tennessee, City of Nashville. I do hereby certify that it has been satisfactorily proved to me, an Alderman in & for

4

said City, by good and lawful testimony that the bearer, James Freeman, a middle-aged dark man, has purchased his freedom and maintained records indicating so. He is upwards of forty five years of age and is six feet three inches high and has several scars on his back and a small scar on the right cheek. James is a good conditioned man and owns real estate in Tennessee and has behaved himself correctly for many years. He is in our opinion, trustworthy and honest. In testimony whereof, I have hereunto affixed my hand & seal at the City of Nashville this 8th day of September in the year of 1824. Signed, William Richardson."

"'Trustworthy and honest.' Not only is he free, but he seems mighty important," said the man, who had been checking the carriage. He now brought his horse alongside his companion's.

"You find anything back there?" the first man asked as he studied the boy's papers.

"Not a lick." He spit more tobacco.

The man placed his hand out and let the papers hit the floor.

"You boys stay out of trouble. We looking for some property belonging to Craig Williamson. You just so happen to fit the physical description. I'd hate to see somethin' happen to you," he said with an evil grin. "Y'all be safe and smile. It's a lovely day, ain't it?"

They turned their horses and rode off down toward Memphis. The father kept his head turned to the rear with his hand fixed near the bag until the two outlines disappeared.

The father hesitated to pick the papers off the floor. He gave the boy his, and the two put them away again. He picked the reins back up and gave the horses a light slap. The two sat silent while the high-pitched melodies of a choir of chickadees filled the quiet air.

Off to the side of the trail, the boy watched an evangelical preacher addressing a group of blacks. Dressed in purple, he stood still and spoke calmly. Around him, the throng of worshippers began to stomp and throw their lank arms high and wide to the heavens. A man armed with a rifle stood some twenty feet away from the group, staying ever vigilant. The boy continued to watch until his father's loud voice broke the silence.

"That is why you NEVER leave home without your papers. Do you hear me?"

"We shouldn't have to do that. Why do we have to explain just breathing? We don't look like no runaways."

The boy had a sour look on his face. His hands had not stopped shaking since the encounter. He was so angry that his stomach began to toss and turn, and he felt as if he would throw up or cry. He hated the situation but was moreover inflamed that he had been afraid during the encounter.

His father replied, "We shouldn't but this is where we are livin.' And until the day comes, we have to play by they rules, but that day is coming."

"You should've shot them." The boy sat back and sulked like a child half his age.

"Oh? Then what? You and me go on the run? To leave your ma and sister and brothers to fend for theyselves while they hang us from a poplar tree?"

The boy did not respond.

"Son, your heart is in the right place, but unless you ready to go to war with them guns they got, you fight in another way until you can get them guns. A man protects his family, and had one of them crackers went to make a move on you or me, I'd waste no time in putting them under. But what you suggestin' is just lookin' for trouble that you not ready to handle."

His father softened his great voice to appeal to the boy who would not have it. Pride, immaturity, and a misunderstanding of what war entails took over him.

"But I am ready to go to war. I'm just as big and strong as any white boy, and don't nothin' give them the right to tell me what I can and can't do. Where we can and can't go!" The tears he had been holding on to escaped his grasp and began to stream down his dark-brown face.

"Sometimes I don't even feel free," he said.

"That's 'cause you don't know what it's like to NOT be free. If you did, you'd be more appreciative."

"But, Paw, you a free man. It don't mean nothin' to you that you can't go where you please? You ain't one of them slaves."

His father pulled back hard on the reins and choked the horses once again. He stared down for a moment. When he turned to look at the boy, he had a grim look on his face that sent a chill down the boy's spine.

"Them slaves is your people. So long as you black and breathin,' don't you look down on them. Them two men coulda took you and made you one of 'them slaves' by the mornin.'"

What almost looked like hatred in the father's eyes appeared to turn them red for a moment. The boy had never seen his father look at him with such disdain, and his tears began to fall even more. He kept his mouth shut and wiped his eyes with his shirt, the tears staining the blue cotton. The entire ride home, his father lectured him on responsibility and maturity. These glided in one of the boy's ears and ejected out of the other.

That night, the boy sat at a table while dinnertime preparations were underway. In front of him sat a spread of cornbread, greens, beans, and chicken, all on a dark-brown oak table. His brooding face stared past the food as if it were not there. His older sister, a beautiful girl of eighteen, set down some forks at each place at the table. Her voice echoed throughout the wooden home as she yelled to their younger brothers. A small brown child of about four walked in the room holding the hand of a brown-skinned chubby boy of about eleven. All the boys were mere copies of the father at the various times in his life.

Their mother walked to the dining room and wiped her hands on her black-and-red flower-patterned dress. Small signs of aging were beginning to appear on her face. A touch of gray dotted her thick, dark hair. Even in her forties, she was still a beautiful, graceful woman. She kissed each of her four children and her husband before she sat down.

The boy's father held out his massive hands, and the family followed suit. He led the family in prayer, thanking God for the food and, most importantly, for family. A loud "Amen" echoed through the house, and food began to pass from person to person. The boy's mother dropped a mound of greens onto his plate. Minutes later, they remained there as he twirled them around his fork, listening to his father. He related their experience earlier in the day to the boy's mother before turning to the boy.

"That is why I always tell you, you get the money and land, and them white folks gots to respect you. See, I didn't have nobody to show me when I was comin' up, but you're smarter now than I'll ever be. When I'm old and gray, you'll run the business mighty fine."

The boy rested his left cheek onto his palm, and only looked up at his father after that statement. He had a long history of never voicing what was on his mind, being too afraid to stand up. He was often paralyzed by the mere thought of his views or statements being wrong. For someone to challenge them was his worst nightmare.

He never wanted to let down his father, for to disappoint his father was to disappoint God. After all, his father knew best and always had. But the boy was now a man, or so he thought. He would have to blaze his own path and walk out of the large shadow that his father cast. Something inside of him screamed to speak up. He was forced to relay his aspirations to his father for the first time. His voice stammered and cracked as he formed the words.

"I don't want to be in real estate."

The boy etched his face in surprise. It was almost as if he had not said the words but heard them come from someone else. His body rose up in the wooden chair and now he sat upright and straight. The weight of those words had been crushing him for quite some time, and his spirit now felt lighter. His father's fork bounced against his plate. The loud clang startled everyone. He looked up at the boy, rubbed the stubble of a graying beard, and spoke.

"And just what do you think you're gonna do?"

"I don't know. I hear New Orleans is good for free colored folk."

A few seconds ago, power and strength permeated through his pores. They were now evaporated as the heat from his father's unrelenting stare shook him to the core.

"You hear that, Anne? The boy wants to go to New Orleans. Why, that's nothin' but a den of sinners," his father barked.

"Why would you leave your family?" his mother asked.

Her soft voice was almost inaudible in comparison to the father's growling baritone. With kind brown eyes, she stared at the boy. Naturally, as a mother she worried for each of her children, but she worried for the boy especially. As she carried him in her womb, she often expressed concern to her husband. That was fifteen long years ago, and only now did she know what she felt.

"I just want to see what's out there," the boy said.

His father scrunched up his face and began to yell even louder.

"What's out there? What's out there ain't nothin' but a bunch of hateful crackas lookin' to toss your hide onto someone's plantation or worse. I was torn from my mama's arms at four years old. Four. And I'll be damned if I watch one of my own do the same by himself."

"But I don't wanna spend my life stuck in some town where any white man can tell me what I can and can't do. That don't make me no man." He cut the words off as soon as he uttered them, knowing that he had gone too far. His father's face contorted in a mix of hurt and anger.

"I ain't a man? I bought my freedom so you can even have yours. I worked my hide raw, day and night, so you could have a better life than bein' treated like a ox in them damn fields, but I ain't a man?"

The boom of his great fists against the table added the exclamation to his question. The boy's youngest brother began to cry, and his mother stood up and went over to the child to pick him up and console him. Terror now seized the boy, and he envied his younger brother. He sat still, wishing his mother would hug and console him as well.

His father was a strong, imposing man. He had seen him pull a wagon out of the mud when an ox failed to do so. He would never raise his hand against his father, but he now felt that his father would not hesitate to do so to him. He could have looked out the window and seen Jesus himself fighting a seven-headed beast, and he would not have been half as frightened as he was of his father at that moment. But still, he refused to back down from his position, even as tears again fell from his eyes.

"I got different plans for my life," he said.

"I ain't heard one plan out of your mouth."

"I wanna travel, maybe be an adventurer and write about it."

"You hear that, Anne? He wants to travel," the father mocked before the boy's mother interrupted.

"Son, all your family is here. The people who love you."

"Let me tell you something," his father interjected. "You ain't nothing without your family, you hear me, boy? I don't care where you go, who you meet, or what you do, without your family you ain't nothing."

The boy's mother spent her time between quieting his crying brother and calming down his father. The boy left the table and went back to his own room, a luxury indeed. He sobbed like a child, with salty tears soaking his pillow. No matter how hard he tried to forget, his father's reddened eyes remained chiseled in his mind. His goal had not been to insult his father, and for this he felt sorry. Though he would not waver in his position nor would he apologize. The amazing relationship he enjoyed with his father was now ruined. The two would never be the same again, the boy thought. Their laughter, jokes, and understanding of each other were now all gone, and he began to sob even more.

After about ten minutes, a different, dangerous thought darted across his mind. Maybe this was for the best? Perhaps his disassociation from his family now meant that he was free to do what he wanted. Of course they would thank him and understand when he had made something of himself. Or perhaps his father was just jealous at the free life the boy wanted to live and his propensity to do so. Yes. That was it, and with that he ceased his crying. His father was jealous and now hated him, so why spend any second more in a home where he was not wanted? Besides, his life was meant to be out there, on the road. He was destined to be where he could live free and not have to answer to any random white man. He grabbed a cowhide knapsack and began to fill it with many items before he stashed it under his bed.

In the dark hours of the night, he grabbed a candle and some paper, sat at the desk in his room, and wrote a note to his mother. He then began the daunting task of getting to the front door. The floorboards, which were silent any other time, now cried out under each step as if they wanted to keep him there. After what seemed to be an hour, he reached the front door. He closed it behind himself without making a sound and stepped outside.

The moon was up high in the sky, and he turned around and looked at his home, which was eerily illuminated by its light. His heart pounded at the dangers that awaited him out there. He could be caught by a gang of ferocious slave catchers and thrown into the back of a wagon, never to be seen again. Or attacked by one of the many black bears that frequented the woods of this area. Yet both of those fears paled in comparison to the thought of the life that awaited him if he stayed home. He looked back at the dark road and found himself frozen with fear.

"Maybe in the morning," he said as he crept, catlike and undetected, back into his home.

He lay motionless on his bed while fantastic thoughts ran through his head. He pictured himself in New Orleans. He saw himself surrounded by a crowd of adventure seekers. They stood at the dock of some ship destined to travel around the tip of South America. The captain would choose him for his large size and strength among men twice his age. The ship would take him to some foreign land where the men's speech sounded like that of dogs. The faceless inhabitants would run to him and adorn him with many gifts. His favorite being their beautiful brown-eyed daughters. The natives would hail him as some king from a faraway land and clothe him in the finest robes and handmade tunics. He would bring these gifts and prizes back to America and stand before dozens to tell of his journeys. Perhaps his family, save his father, would come with him to this place of true freedom.

By the time he was ready to catch some sleep, it was already early in the morning. He needed to leave now or else put it off for another day. Facing his father today was not an option, and he again made his way past the floorboards and out the front door. He remembered the story of Lot's wife, who was turned into salt after looking back at the destruction of Sodom and Gomorrah, and this time he would not turn his head to see his home. The coming sun would soon light the countryside and banish any demons from his path. He walked strong and upright down the tree-lined path for an hour before his heart dropped to his stomach. He reached into his knapsack and tossed his hand around. He grabbed the tin that contained his freedom papers. He clutched onto it, then placed it gently into the sack as if it were glass, and he resumed his walk going west on that warm summer morning.

2

A Forsaken Soul

I n the year 1825, a fifteen-year-old would find no trouble in leaving home and obtaining an occupation. The boy traveled back to Memphis before working as a porter on a steamboat. He began his travels down the Mighty Mississippi toward New Orleans. To his surprise, he was surrounded by a host of free blacks who worked as cooks, barbers, and waiters. They fared much better than their on-land counterparts, as they were paid both wages and tips. These blacks often found themselves at odds with laborers from Germany and Ireland. These groups would often quarrel with one another and fight almost daily.

The river's scenery fascinated the boy's eyes and mind. He would see hordes of cottonwood trees, so numerous that even God himself couldn't know their number. Viewers waved at the boat from bluffs that towered forty feet over the river. Six- to eight-foot-long alligators sunbathed on the open areas of the shore. The largest cotton plantations he had ever seen sat on the shores near Vicksburg, Mississippi, becoming more numerous as they continued. Gaunt, black bodies spread out among the fields, stooped over with humps in their backs. Hung around their necks were tan sacks that were filled with fluffy white gold. On certain nights, the sounds of banjos came from their rundown cabins and twirled their way over to the docked ship while the passengers danced and stomped along to the faint rhythm.

A week and a half from the time he left home, the boy arrived in New Orleans. When he was younger, his grandmother proclaimed him to be "a child of the world." As he stared at this strange new realm, he was dead set on making this declaration ring true.

"Let's get these bales moving, boys," said a man standing at the bottom of the ramp. His red face glistened with sweat, and he adjusted his glasses.

An agitated group of men stood on the deck, waiting for their turns to transport the cotton to land. The blacks stood together in one area, segregated from their white counterparts. The groups splintered off into various conversations of indistinct chatter. The boy spoke to an older man named Moses.

"I been all up and down this river. You see, the key is to play dumb and listen to them," said Moses.

"What do you mean?" said the boy.

"They don't think nothin' of us Negroes and can't think of a Negro bein' smart enough to listen and understand what they talkin' about. I know a guy, name is Johnny Porter, and he worked as a waiter on a fancy ship. Them white folks would always be talkin' about what they gonna do with they money and how to get more of it. He just followed what they did and bought some land with a saltpeter mine on it. Saltpeter the thing they use in gunpowder, and he got rich just from that."

The boy was silent.

"I been savin' up my money, and I'm gone buy me some coal or a whole coal mine," said Moses.

"Coal? What you gonna do with that?"

"I'm gone buy it for a low price during the summer. Then, when winter come 'round, and they need it, I'll sell it for triple the price."

"That actually ain't a bad idea," the boy said.

"I know it ain't. I'm the one that came up with it."

"But where you gonna store it? How you gonna transport it?"

"Oh hush. I ain't gonna let you throw salt on my fire. You nothin' but a boy no way, what do you know? All I need is one good white man to buy it for me."

"What you need a white man for? Why we always 'need a white man'? You can't do that yourself?" the boy asked.

Moses set down his end of the cart and turned around to look at the boy. Sweat glistened on his dark skin. The boy stood up straight, and they looked at each other eye to eye. Moses's blood red eyes told of either a lack of a night's rest or the fifty years that he had spent working day in and day out.

"Fool, do you know where we livin'? Without a white man's help, they don't let a Negro have nothing."

The boy disagreed, though he hid from conflict and kept any further arguments to himself. He hadn't developed any concrete thoughts of his own to stand on and, like most boys his age, was unsure of himself. The irony being that the previous week, he had stood up to his father, but here he was giving more respect to a stranger.

The line had moved farther along by now. When it was their turn to exit the boat, another cart, guided by two white men, swerved in front of them. They almost hit Moses, who yelled out and then shut his mouth, as if he immediately regretted it.

"Best for you boys to watch where you be headin'," said one of the men in a thick Irish accent. He raised his hat slightly to reveal sharp brown eyes. He and the boy entered an intense staring match. The Irishman took this as an insult and became more agitated the more the boy looked into his eyes.

The boy would often daydream about moments such as this. In those dreams, he would stand up tall and stare the perpetrator in the eyes. From the pit of his gut, a response would arise that would liberate his soul from the cage it felt trapped in. This comeback was almost always followed by a punch, kick, or stab of some sort. Upon which the white offender would comically crawl away to whatever hole he came from. The blacks around the boy would hoist him high onto their shoulders and parade him around town as a hero.

Before the boy could decide to do none of these things, a small group of blacks put down their carts and walked over to join him and Moses. A group of whites did likewise and assembled behind the Irishman. The groups exchanged harsh, unforgivable words, and the inevitable cursing and shoving began.

Back on land, a crowd formed and watched the tussle, looking giddy with excitement. A group of commissioned vigilante officers rushed on board and began to separate the men. After several whacks of their clubs on the blacks, they were able to restore order. Both groups returned to their carts and continued the operation as normal. The Irishman shot the boy a menacing, hateful glance. He said something inaudible to his partner before they left the boat.

"Why don't you ask them for help with your coal?" asked one of the black men. The entire group laughed, picked up their carts, and began to walk toward the ramp.

Hours later, the sun had begun to set and the sky cast an amazing pinkish, orange glow on the city of New Orleans. The city was a virtual melting pot. People of Haitian, French, German, Polish, and Italian descent all flocked there. Just outside of the city lived a less-favored group. Captive souls were forced to work on the massive sugar and cotton plantations. Slave labor was the backbone of the nation's economy, and New Orleans led as a prime example of its profitability.

The boy and Moses stood side by side on the edge of a large field, their shadows long and distorted. On the field, a team of free blacks played a game of raquette against a team of blacks and Choctaw Natives. There looked to be about fifty men on each team; in the chaos it was hard to be sure. Like ants swarming toward a dead beetle, they ran around with their rackets, trying to toss a ball into a small goalpost. The boy had never seen, nor heard, of the sport. It would have bored him were it not for the frequent and deliberate blows to the head, shin, and body. One man received a stiff hit to his nose. He rolled around the field, covering it with blood splattered everywhere. A horde of men waited for their chance to join the game. One ran over to the man and helped him off the field. He then picked up his stick and replaced him without saying a word. Unbeknownst to the boy, as he stood laughing and joking, he was being watched from across the wide field.

After about five more minutes, the boy wanted to see more of the city and excused himself and went to find an outhouse. He walked and overheard conversations in French, Spanish, and English. He heard a Native language that sounded like the speakers had pebbles in their mouths. Every so often he tripped on a raised piece of the brick-laid street, making his walk that much more awkward. On either side of him were beautifully colored two- and three-story buildings. The colors, stucco, and ironwork were all testaments to the recent Spanish presence in the city.

He began to feel nervous and tense and had been expecting someone to come to him and ask to see his papers. His uneasiness showed all over his face as he stared at people who often stared back, though they perhaps were more interested in that strange walk of his than his skin color or freedom status. He walked on his toes with an awkward spring in his step. Tall, lank, and black, he would have attracted attention even if he were not bouncing around town.

After five minutes of wandering, he came to an inn. Red bricks made up the outside of the building, many of which were missing or chipped. It looked as if it had not seen a respectable customer since it opened. Tucked away behind the inn was a small, rundown outhouse. The area was so quiet that he felt as if he were violating some unwritten rule by entering. He poked his head around and walked the area like a dog before he felt safe enough to use it. He opened the wooden door of the jakes. A rancid smell attacked his nostrils, causing him to jump back. When he gathered himself, he stepped inside and closed the latch behind him.

When he finished, he pushed open the door, eager for fresh air. He was met by the stare of a man who was about twenty feet away; it was the Irishman. The boy had been looking down and caught glimpse of the man's long shadow, which sat two feet from him. The shadow held a large, six-foot machete. When the boy looked up, it was no more than a six-inch knife that the man twirled in his hand as if he were playing with a toy. He held a sinister look in his eye, and the boy knew that this was not a game and indeed was very serious.

The boy had been standing halfway in the jakes and halfway out when he saw the man. He almost fell backward and had to take control of his legs. The sun was setting behind the Irishman. With the contrast of light, he appeared to be some dark figure from the boy's nightmares. The two stood and stared at each other before the boy spoke.

"W–What do you want?"

"Simple. Respect that's owed to me."

"Well, you got that. Nothin' happened, and we can both go about our lives."

"We could, but there's one wee little problem. I would always look back and kick me self, knowing that I didn't put a nigger back in his place. If I'm not man enough to do even that, I couldn't live with me self."

He took slow, deliberate steps toward the boy. The boy's legs quivered, and he could not move. He waited for the fearlessness he believed was in himself to rise up, but it did not come. He looked past the man, hoping to see someone that he could yell to for help, but he found no one.

His mind shifted to the story his mother had told him about his grandfather, from many years ago. An overseer had made an attempt at his wife. When he confronted the overseer, the man attacked him. His grandfather caught the whip, beat the man to within inches of his life, and left him bedridden for months. Such was the blood that pumped through the boy's veins. He figured that if an enslaved man could muster the strength to fight, then he for sure could do the same. He exited the jakes. His limbs moved so slow that it looked as though they were locked in one position for years. He took up an attacking stance and prepared himself.

The Irishman was much shorter than the boy but had big legs, wide shoulders, and looked to be strong. His confidence shined through as he lunged at the boy with the knife. The boy sidestepped and caused him to miss. They performed similar dance steps for about thirty seconds before the man looked up at him. His face was red with frustration as he spoke.

"I'll make a deal with ye. I mark your cheek, and we call it square."

The boy thought about the concession for a moment. It was better to leave with a scar on his cheek than to leave in a coffin. In this confrontation with a white man, he knew that no matter the circumstance, he would be at fault. As soon as he began to open his mouth, the man jumped at him again, this time only narrowly missing.

The boy kept his mouth shut and now maintained his distance and focused all attention on the blade. A few months ago, his father had given him a flintlock pistol and a knife. An old Cherokee woman crafted the knife and gifted it to the boy's father, who gave it to him. But both these items were with his belongings at the hotel. He panicked as he searched through his mind for a way out of this situation.

Without hesitation, the Irishman ran toward him again. The boy easily dodged the lackluster swing. The man then bent down and grabbed hold of the boy's torso and drove him to the grass. The boy landed on his back and immediately began to panic. The Irishman was on top of him and swung the knife down through the humid air. The slash against the boy's right cheek gave a hot sensation but did not immediately register any pain. The boy had turned his head to the left to avoid any major damage. The Irishman raised the knife high above his head.

With his head turned, the boy saw a large stone. He grabbed it with his left hand, and with all the force he could muster, he swung it at the Irishman's head. The collision caused a loud clacking noise that the entire city had to have heard. The handle of the Irishman's knife bounced on the boy's chest. The man who once held it fell like a doll to the boy's right side. His face hit the ground, and he did not move. He lay there with eyes wide open, staring at the dirt. The boy was still on his back, looking up at the sky. His chest rose and fell in quick, short spurts for a moment before he turned over and made his way to his hands and knees.

"Are you quits?" he asked while dabbing at the trickle of hot blood on his face.

Strength and valor filled his spirit. He stood up with an air of honor about himself, having defended himself and acted out his daydreams. Now he would help the man up. Perhaps they would go grab a drink together. The drunk man would express ignorance and regret at how wrong he had been.

But the man did not respond. His mouth had been shut forever. The boy looked down at him and noticed the huge gash etched onto his temple. Blood spurted out of the wound, soaking his shirt, hair, and the dirt around him.

Feelings of triumph evaporated, and shocking fear began to rain down on the boy. Terror seized his body, and he felt as if he would faint. His heart turned into a pounding African drum, the likes of which could be heard miles away. His eyes were open wide and his mouth agape as he stared at the body.

"Please, God, please please please. Don't be dead. Please, God, no!"

He pleaded with the Almighty to save him. But God has never fulfilled such requests, not even for his favorite souls. The boy continued to beg, switching between talking to God and the man. He turned the man over onto his back, and his body lay flat like a rug, his eyes now staring past the sky. The boy placed his hands on the man's wrists to check for a pulse but felt none.

Scenarios ran through the boy's mind, and they all ended with a rope around his neck. Large salty tears began to form in his eyes and fell on the man's face as the boy started to frantically shake him. He pumped his hands on the man's chest and even tried resuscitation. Of course none of this worked, and the man lay still. His soul slowly drifting to whichever afterworld would claim it first. He knelt over the man and cried for what seemed to be an eternity.

Survival instincts kicked in, and he knew that he had to hide the body before someone came to the area. He easily dragged the man, what was once the man, behind the outhouse. He tossed the body among the thick vegetation where it couldn't easily be seen. The stone the boy had used sat innocent and looked to be any other rock. The boy cursed it and placed it into the latrine pit of the outhouse. He slammed the door shut, looked around, and still saw no one. Then he began a half run, half walk down Orleans Street. He passed the cathedral, with its large white spires that dominated the skyline. As it towered over him, he felt that somehow the church itself was staring at him. It was judging him, and he sped past it even faster.

The innkeeper and his wife were alone in the foyer of their humble establishment. He pushed the glasses up on his round, dark face and showed his perfect set of teeth in response to a joke she made. She was standing on a chair while dusting a painting of the Haitian coastline when the doors of the inn burst open. By the time either realized what had happened, the boy had rushed through the foyer and up to his room. He rustled around the room to retrieve all his belongings. Before the innkeeper's wife could steady herself and calm down, the boy was out of the inn as quickly as he had come. The two stood with puzzled looks on their faces. The boy did not say a word to them, nor did he attempt to find Moses, whom he would never see again.

He followed the river north, continuously moving the whole way. He passed several inns and public gardens; small one-story homes crafted out of mud with thatched roofs that hung over the side of them; a road of two-story mansions with lamps that dangled over the streets.

At some spots he ran, while at others he made a speedy walk. His breaths were heavy, his legs were weighed down with lead and he worried that they would give out. Trails of throw-up every so often followed his path, as he never stopped moving. He had become so discombobulated that he had not realized that it was now nighttime and that he, in fact, could not see in front of him. Clouds concealed the moon and not even his nose was visible to him. He reached for a tree and rubbed his hands on the rough crevices of the bark. He slid down to his butt and leaned against it, taking short, quick breaths like some wounded animal. His chest was ready to explode, and he began to cry, and soon he slept like a child.

3

Rough Waters

E arly the next morning, swarms of insects buzzed on and around his face. One large beetle in particular misjudged its flight and knocked against his lip. The collision felt like a small rock had hit him, and woke him up. When he opened his puffy eyes, he panicked at not being able to see out of them. He wiped the dried tears on the collar of his linen shirt and looked up at the small creek that was barely visible through the tall grass in front of him. He blew the contents of his nose into the grass next to him and swatted at the insects.

His heart pumped, and he thanked God that what he experienced was nothing more than a long, bad dream. He was sure that he had fallen asleep on his parents' land while working. He looked around and hoped to see his mother fetching eggs from their chicken coop. He wished to see his younger brothers making a game of the pellets they often threw at them. But his heart broke as he stared at the blankets of loose Spanish moss that draped from the trees.

He remembered the blank stare of the dead Irishman and

realized he was far from Tennessee. He began to pray out loud that none of this was real, but reality is rarely what we desire it to be. A man was dead at his hands. Now he was running from what was sure to be his own death. Self-defense or not, he knew his life would never be the same again.

He stood up and, like the day before, began to run again. By now, he knew that he was heading north to Baton Rouge, where he could catch a steamboat going upriver. Curious blacks, clothed in tattered rags, watched him from the isolated plantations. He slowed his pace to a quick walk, and a strange feeling came over him. He dropped to the ground and stuck his left ear to the dirt. A faint vibration began to increase in intensity.

From the south, a black carriage raced toward him. He sprung to the side of the road into the vegetation like a jackrabbit. While crouched down in murky water, the mud began to pull his feet downward into the earth until he was ankle deep in it. In his right hand, he clutched the pistol. His body was snakelike, tightly coiled and ready to strike. A well-dressed black driver whipped the reins viciously. Two white occupants stared deep at the side of the road. They saw nothing but the tall foliage that stuck out of the water while only God knows what lurked beneath.

The boy took his time to emerge from the thicket and continue his journey. An inner struggle took root, and the boy began to unravel mentally as thoughts swirled in his mind. He started to not only speak out loud but to also respond to himself as if another person were present.

"I had to kill him," he wailed. "He was going to kill me."

"No, you didn't. You took it too far."

"No, no, no. He was just out of it from the blood loss. Maybe somebody found him, and he woke up and won't remember. This whole thing won't amount to much."

"Fool, he's dead. At your hands. You wanted to leave home so bad, now look at you."

Home. The utterance of this word stopped him in his tracks.

"I can't go back there."

Tears gushed from his swollen eyes and dripped off his chin onto the ground. Only now that he stopped did he take notice of the pain in his feet and legs. To escape it, he began to walk again and continued to speak to himself. His dark side won the argument, and he gave up the self-defense angle. He knew now that his soul was damned and that God had turned his back on him.

But if God knew all, and all things were written, wouldn't this be God's fault? Why wouldn't God intervene? A large egret that had been watching him as he ranted to himself took flight and left. The boy took this as a sign that God had indeed left him. Nothing but the wind moved around the boy, who stood still with his head spinning. He was alone now, and fear closed in around him as he wondered where his soul would rest when he was to die.

"The devil ain't too far," his grandmother would always say.

Now that he was without God's protection, he was sure that he would find out soon if that statement were true.

That night he sat again in the wilderness with no fire. His head turned up at the sky, not sure if his eyes were open or closed. Once more, he cried himself to sleep. A small part of him actually welcomed any beast or demon to come and put an end to his suffering.

The next day, a shell of a human trudged through the dirt roads and into the city of Baton Rouge. On tired and weary feet, he made his way to a port. He found a Cajun man that was offering passage to Natchez, Mississippi, on a flatboat. The short, fat man looked perplexed when the boy gave him double the fare, but he asked no questions. The two did not speak any more that day as they made their way up the river. At night he slept with his head hung down and almost looked to be at peace, though a battle raged in his mind.

The next morning, he opened his eyes and saw the endless trees that dominated the banks of the river. When the Cajun saw that he was up, he spoke to him.

"Is everything all right with you friend?"

He looked at the man through clouded eyes.

"I must've been talking in my sleep."

The Cajun slicked back his balding hair into a ponytail.

"How you talk, sounded like you done a murder of some sort. How you 'didn't mean to.' News travels fast on this river, and I don't want no trouble here."

"You ain't in none," the boy said as he rubbed his eyes.

The Cajun wiped his pink forehead with a blue kerchief and stared at the boy.

"All right, friend, we'll be there shortly."

The boy again hoped this was all a dream and again was disappointed. He did not look up again, nor did he move until the Cajun called out for Natchez. The boy made a hasty exit and wasted no time in hiring himself out onto another steamboat.

The ship was constructed the previous year in New York. The oak wood still emitted faint odors of what smelled to be urine. One hundred and fifty feet long and complete with an upper and lower deck, the ship impressed all who saw it. Day after day, in port after port, merchandise and passengers entered and exited the ship.

The upper deck beheld affluent men and women who enjoyed warmth on those cold river nights. They sat around feeling mighty and important, sipping glasses of imported wine.

On the lower deck, bales of cotton and crates of sugar and molasses towered over the wooden floors. They were packed tightly together, making it difficult to move among them. Also on this deck was a small herd of cattle, whining goats, and a few oxen that looked ready to jump ship at any moment. Sharing quarters with these annoyances were the more indigent passengers. These commuters covered every inch of the deck. If the foul odor of the animals didn't churn one's stomach, the scent of two hundred unwashed bodies sure would. At night, men, women, and children of all races and nationalities huddled together for warmth. It was among these travelers that the boy would sleep. His back against bales of cotton that were bound for New York, Pittsburgh, and Boston.

After about a week, the boat came to and then passed Memphis. His family had not ceased to look for him since the day he left, and he did not venture out into the city upon their stop there. He feared that either the authorities or his family put out descriptions of him.

In his anger, he began to blame his loved ones for his misfortunes. If they had let him do what he pleased, he never would have run away, and his hands would be free from the blood. He would have still left home but under different circumstances. Why couldn't they understand his desire to travel and not live stuck as his father was?

It was quite ironic that his desire to travel was possible only due to the job and lifestyle his father led. The encyclopedias that expanded his horizons were very difficult for a black man to come by. Several sat in the boys' room, informing him of life outside of the United States. However, his young mind could not grasp this.

North of Memphis, he sat alone at a clearing overlooking the muddy waters. Out in front of him, black men in canoes joked and laughed as they rowed over to a large piece of driftwood. They looked up at the boy and threw their hands up in acknowledgement but received no reply. He engaged in conversation with himself. He was sure that now the body was discovered. He berated himself for running through the city, which was an admission of guilt. He concluded that he couldn't go home and resolved to continue farther north.

He sat and waited for the tears to fall. He strained as best as he could to conjure up thoughts of sadness and loneliness. When he realized that he could not cry anymore, his stare became blank and nonchalant. He felt that the warmth of his soul had been ripped out, leaving him hollow and cold. Before, the tears had helped remind him of the regret he felt. Now, without them, he knew what it was like to be an animal, capable of killing with no remorse. General sadness and hopelessness collected, and hovered over him in a dark cloud. Without a vent, these feelings would soon give rise to other, dangerous outlets.

At four in the morning, the captain decided to get an early start on the day. He firmly gripped the mahogany wheel and his voice echoed throughout the dark as he gave the call to ship out. The lights on board illuminated very little outside of the ship's radius. The minimal amount of moonlight made the river navigable only to watchful eyes. At times, large chunks of driftwood would bang and scratch against the hull of the ship. The noise would send the ever-incessant animals into a frenzy, which would drown out the loud clicking sounds that radiated from the boilers below.

The boy again slept against bales of cotton with his knapsack firmly secure in his arms. He felt a nudge on his foot that he was sure had been a part of his dream. A second nudge woke him up, and an old man leered at him through pale blue eyes. Filthy, gray hair ran down to his shoulders, which were covered by the rags of overalls, much the same color. A long, dirty beard bounced as he spoke.

"I know who you are."

The old man's back sat against cotton bales as well. He pulled his feet back into their original cross-legged position. His boots, dry and cracked, looked to have been the first pair ever crafted.

With no room to walk between the two, the boy jumped, as the old man had not been there when the boy fell asleep.

"I think you got the wrong guy," the boy said.

"I wasn't sure until you looked up, and I seen that there scar. The news traveled quicker than you did."

"I don't know about nothin' you're talking about."

"That's where you wrong. You see, I know you do, and I also know by the pitiful look on your face and the whimperin' you did in your sleep, that this was the first man you done killed."

With only the light from the small gas lamps, the man's sunburnt face was only faintly illuminated. Movement near the man's waist caught the boy's attention, and he looked down to see a large pistol trained on him. He looked around at the various families that were all strewn about. A mother rubbed her daughter's head and softly sung her to sleep.

"You ain't gone shoot me right here," he said.

"Just give me the reason. They put fifty dollars on your head, so you just stay there nice and quiet like, and at the next stop, let's say you and me get off real peaceful."

The boy had two choices: to attack the old man or to surrender. At the conclusion of either choice, he pictured his skinny body swinging from a tree, his eyeballs so large that they appeared ready to pop out of their sockets. Panic began to set in as he searched for some way out of this scenario. He considered jumping overboard and swimming to the west bank of the shore. There he would go on the run in Arkansas Territory, but how would he survive in that unforgiving region?

Then, as if by some ironic act of providence, one of the three boilers exploded on the floor beneath them. The ship rocked as if a piece of artillery had hit it. Shards of metal rocketed every which way, slicing through the air. Some pieces were later found stuck in trees on shore, almost a quarter of a mile away. The ejected boiler door spun violently and found a new home in the stomach of a Mississippian man, nearly cutting him in half. The shock flung several travelers from the deck into the river. Large bales of cotton displaced and tumbled down onto passengers. The immense weight crushed limbs, torsos, and even heads of adults and children alike. Those who weren't crushed were hurled clear across the deck.

The gust of air from the explosion raced around the boat and extinguished all light on board. Passengers dragged their feet around and tripped over dead or dying bodies in the dark. Parents yelled for their terrified children, who screamed back in horror. The shouts of men from below decks drowned out all else as they cried for help that would arrive too late.

A tall Georgian man slid with caution across the deck toward the only source of light. He came to and fell down into one of the blown-off hatchways. He howled in pain at the scalding water that rose up to his knees. Frantically, he jumped up and down, attempting to grab a hold of anything to pull himself up.

By now, the boy's eyes had begun to adjust to the dark. He stood up and slowly began to walk, tripping over several dead bodies in his way. He reached the rope that hung on the wall at the center of the ship and quickened his pace to the hatchway. He tossed the rope down to the screaming man and told him to grab hold. By now, several other men scooted over to the boy and helped him pull the man up to safety. His flesh was badly burned off his legs, and a soft sizzling noise came from them. As if the scene couldn't get any more chaotic, shouts of fire came from the few survivors below.

The first lifeboat was dropped, and women and small children reached out to their husbands and fathers with tears in their eyes. Guided by lanterns, a man started to row the boat toward a small clearing on the eastern bank of the Mississippi. Once he reached it and the first wave of survivors was let off, he began the arduous process of returning to the ship. The passengers began to panic even more after seeing how slow the process was going. Many elected to jump ship and took their chances with the river's current.

The captain emerged from the pilot house with serious eyes and clutched the railing. A man of about forty, he looked to have been on the water all his life. He remained calm and cool under pressure as he yelled out to the crew members who were still on board.

"Toss the cotton," he said.

The bales plunged into the murk with loud splashes. They bobbed up and down with the current, waiting for men to swim to them to use as flotation devices.

Fire now illuminated the ship. The heat from it was somewhat comforting on that cold night. The boy felt rushed to get off the ship. He feared that another boiler would explode at any moment, worse than the first.

Just fifteen minutes earlier, he thought that he would have welcomed death. Now that he felt the heat of it on his skin, he realized he was not ready to die. He tossed his knapsack over his shoulder and made his way to the ship's railing. As he went to climb and jump, a strong hand grabbed his shoulder. It spun him around and delivered a halfhearted punch to his mouth. The old man's eyes pierced and beheld the light of the fire that was a mere thirty feet to his left. He threw another punch, which the boy ducked.

"The boat's going down. We have to get off it," the boy said.

"After I tie you up!" the old man said with rope in his left hand.

All his life, the boy was made to answer to whites. The false accusation of any white person, no matter how lowly, could end his life. Being forced to explain his presence no matter where he was had planted a deep-seated resentment in him that began to bloom. His blood began to boil as the part of his grandfather that resided within him began to heat up. A low-pitched growl leaked from him. He rushed the old man and knocked him five feet from where he stood. He jumped on top of him and, with thunderous punches, he began to repeatedly bounce the man's head from left to right. He intended to only subdue the man and give himself time to escape, but he snapped, and when he came to, blood oozed out of the man's mouth.

All around, the passengers were so preoccupied that none saw what was going on. The boy stood, and blood dripped from his knuckles into a growing pool on the deck floor. He grabbed the old man's arm and attempted to help him rise, but his body was limp. He was not dead, but he was knocked out and disoriented. The blaze came closer and with it, the increasing heat. He picked up the old man and supported his small frame on his shoulder as he dragged him over to the edge of the boat. With great difficulty, he got himself and the man over the railing and jumped.

The frigid water seized hold of his muscles, and he lost his grip of the old man. He flung his arms every which way and turned his head from side to side, as if he could actually see down there. After fifteen more seconds, his lungs began to thump the inside his chest and begged for air. He emerged from the water, and he made his way to and grabbed a hold of one of the cotton bales. He coughed violently and wiped his eyes with his free hand. Over on shore, the survivors had already begun a small fire to warm themselves, as the large blaze of the boat lit that entire section of the river valley. The rescue boat now had two fresh rowers, and the boy clung to the cotton until they came to him. He was hysterical as he spoke.

"There was an old man. I tried to save him."

"I know, son. He wasn't the only one," said one of the men rowing the boat as they made their way to another bale.

The boy coughed and shook water out of his ears. He shivered in the cold, but something refocused his attention and warmed him. He madly reached into his soaked knapsack and flung his hand around in the bag. He pushed aside the drenched pistol, the knife, and a compass and pulled out his tin of papers. He flicked the water off, opened it, and made a sigh of relief at the sight of the neatly folded papers that sat inside. As soon as he relaxed, his body began to shiver again, as the cold again took the top priority in his mind.

When the boat arrived at the shore, the mass of survivors cried and wailed. A man held back his wife, who was hell-bent on plunging into the water and saving their daughter. By now her body was half a mile down the river. Other more fortunate families kissed their loved ones and sent praises to God at the sight of their faces. The boy stood alone and watched the boat as another boiler exploded. The lifeboat had still been making trips, and one of the rowers was hit and killed by a metal shard. By now, the boy realized the old man would not emerge. He cursed as he watched the river slowly swallow the fireball of a ship.

4

A Parade of Hopefuls

Several hours later, the sun shined its light on a steamboat that picked up survivors. The savior boat dropped them back off in Memphis. The boy wasted no time in finding employment on yet another steamboat that took off the next day. The boy stayed on guard, though time passed without incident. A week later, he'd made it to St. Louis. Several well-to-do-looking men and women stood among lovely garden terraces and watched the ship come in.

The boy lugged around the city, hunched over with the weight of another murder on his conscience. Frenchmen and Natives loitered idly outside of old French trade houses. They watched him and whispered to themselves as he walked down the long main street that paralleled the river. He wandered past the two-story brick homes owned by wealthy Americans who moved there after the Louisiana Purchase.

At night, filthy and putrid, he would drink his weight in whiskey in some saloon. His head would be plastered to the wooden tables while gruff men rummaged through his pockets. Soon, he could be found behind buildings, surrounded by gangs of undesirable men. Hunters from Kentucky, with long rifles strapped across their backs and large bowie knives on their waists, screamed and yelled at and for him. Straggly Virginians clapped and hooted at the promise of violence. Whenever he was knocked away, the men would push and shove him back into the center of a makeshift ring. His shirtless opponent of the night waited for him, howling like some barbarous animal.

His breath by now had begun to continually reek of alcohol. Anyone within a five-foot radius of him knew without a doubt that he was present. His hair was a mess, and he now "looked as if no one loved him," as his mother would say. He slept where he could, when he could. Sometimes he reclined against wooden buildings. The boisterous sounds of billiard balls, fiddles, and drunken revelry seeming to have no effect on him. At other times, he was just outside of town. His lifeless body lay in between rows of corn, the vermin running across him as if they were playing some game. After a few weeks, he took up residence in a small clearing alongside the Mississippi. His eating, sleeping, and drinking habits made even the wild beasts give him a second glance.

One morning, he lay under his jacket, coiled up with his hands between his knees. A splash of foul-smelling water hit his face and jolted him awake. Without opening his eyes, he blindly reached over to a large stone. He grabbed his grimy, torn shirt and began to wipe his face and naked chest. He quickly sat up straight. His head pounded, as if he had been struck with a billy club, and he slithered back to the ground. He twisted his sore neck and could not remember the kick to his jaw the night before that had made it so. Still with his eyes closed, he scanned the ground with his hands. When he found his slimy hat, he covered his face from the August sun and lay back down.

Another splash of water hit him and knocked off his hat, but this time the boy sat up and did not move. His eyes adjusted to the light, and he gave an evil stare to a man who stood tall and formal. His blue overalls were neat and looked to be brand new, as did his boots, which were in tip-top condition, dirtied only by the silt from the banks of the river. He removed his hat, and the sun gleamed off the perfect dome that was his bald head.

"What the hell you want? I ain't doing nothin' wrong," the boy said.

"Is that so? All this drinkin,' fightin', and carryin' on ain't wrong?"

"Who are you, and what are you watching me for?"

"Hell, I ain't. But I happen to trip over your drunk body almost every place I go. Sleeping outside with the rats and bathin' like you ain't one of God's children. Have you no people, son?"

The man's facial expression transformed. Contempt and disgust turned into a genuine concern and even hurt. The boy did not notice. He stared off at the river and then hung his aching head between his knees. The man looked over at the embers of the boy's fire. The bones of a half-eaten catfish sat on a large, flat rock that had been used as a plate. The man spoke again.

"My name is Walter Linwood, and I'm a blacksmith here in town. You seem to have fallen on some rough times, but that ain't nothin' the good Lord can't patch up."

"That son of a bitch ain't gone patch up nothing.'"

Walter almost jumped back at this expression. His face contorted as he stared at the boy, who still had his head between his knees.

"Don't ever curse the Lord in my presence."

"Well, Walter, I ain't in your presence. You in mine."

The boy looked up and his gaze met the man's, though he appeared to stare past him. Perhaps at the rushing water of the Mississippi that raced southward behind him. His red eyes still clung on to a semblance of innocence. He looked as though he could either cry or lash out in anger at any moment. After a long silence, the man spoke again.

"Sometimes, when you hit a snag in life, all you need is the help of those that care for you."

"What do you care for me? You don't even know my name."

"You haven't given it, and I care more than you know. That's why I stuck my head in your business with the hopes of helpin' you get saved."

"I ain't gettin' saved. I've gone too far." The seriousness of the conversation sobered him up.

"There ain't a hole you can fall into that He won't reach down and pull you up from . . . You was born free? I can hear it in how you talk."

"Ain't no Negro ever truly free in this country. No matter where you go, you gotta answer to some white man, free or not."

"Damn it all if I don't agree on that, son, but will you let me help ye?" He had a look of desperation on his face, as if the answer could make or break his heart.

Salvation was the furthest thing from the boy's mind. Still, he had grown tired of the long, cold nights where insects and animals shared quarters with him. He agreed to this man's "help."

His hand dwarfed Walter's as he assisted him to get on his feet. He faced the sun and stretched out, his arms high above him. He dusted off his brown pants and gathered his meager belongings. The two walked back to Walter's small, humble home that was little more than a shack on the outside of the city. Over the next month, Walter, having no children of his own, began to treat the boy like a son. Walter had begun to divulge information about himself and his wife. She lived on a plantation five miles outside of St. Louis, waiting for him to purchase her freedom.

Both parties enjoyed the distraction that the other provided. Day after day, the boy stood in front of a blazing furnace with Walter and learned the trade of a blacksmith. His mind was so preoccupied with all the fresh opportunities that this environment handed him that he did not have the time to ponder on anything else. For a few weeks, his taste and need for alcohol diminished. It appeared that his life was on an upward trajectory.

This progress, however, was short-lived, as his past began a slow emergence from a shallow grave. His troubled soul could not run forever, and like a siren to a shipwrecked crew, the alcohol and violence of the saloons began to call out to him. The call was quiet at first, faint, even, like a whispering wind. Eventually, it began to scream at him. It seized him, and he was soon reeking of whiskey, fighting in the middle of a ring like a gamecock.

One night in particular, he stood across the circle from an older white man. The man removed his hat and slicked back his graying hair. He removed his buckskin shirt, revealing an aged yet still solid body. He looked over at the boy and grinned through yellow, crooked teeth. The brute banged his huge, crusted knuckles together. A hideous-looking crowd roared in anticipation at the match. A man carrying a beaver-felt hat went to each man in the unappealing crowd. They placed their bets as the man yelled exaggerations and outright lies about the two combatants. His partner, a small man in suspenders, stood between the two prizefighters. His great voice, which did not fit its owner, carried across the town as he spoke.

"I would like to welcome you, gentleman, and any ladies lurking in attendance, to another night of combat. Standing to my left, born in the woods of Delaware, where his mother died during childbirth leaving him to deliver himself unto the world, is the Old Gator, aged but still dangerous, Roger Smith!"

The crowd applauded and chanted his name.

"And to my right . . ."

A perplexed and embarrassed look shot across his face as he leaned in toward the boy and asked where he was from. The boy's reply didn't seem to satisfy the man, and he again spoke.

"Hailing from Mogo Valley in the far reaches of the dark African province of Senegal, a place where few enter and even fewer live to tell about it, this young man is a relative newcomer to the scene and has whooped on every challenger placed against him. Don't let his age or race fool you, give it up for a man known only as the 'Black Baby-Faced Assassin'!"

The boos of the whites drowned out the cheers of the blacks, who screamed at the top of their lungs for "their guy." The referee sent both fighters back to the edge of the ring and asked if either was ready. When they responded positively, he clapped his hands, and the crowd screamed.

The fight started with the boy keeping his distance from the shorter, sturdier-built man. The man threw a wild overhand punch with all his might. The boy sidestepped to the left and threw a right hand of his own that connected with the man's jaw and pushed him back a few feet. The crowd became giddy, and a group of men who had been drinking at one of the saloons ran over like children to join tonight's main form of entertainment. The old man came closer to the boy, stomped hard on his foot, and gave the boy a strong shove. The boy was still falling toward the ground when the old man pounced. They landed in the dirt together with the old man on top of him. He wailed strong, thunderous punches, the same way a man half his age would have.

The booming strikes cut and bruised the boy's already damaged face, and he knew he could not take many more of these. The boy bucked his hips up and tossed the old man forward. With a push, he was able to wiggle from under the man and made his way back to his feet, though he stumbled for a moment. He spit a glob of blood to the edge of the circle, which came close to a man's foot. The two fighters now began to circle each other, hunched over and snarling like feral cats. Each had a look of murder in his eyes and wore menacing smiles as if they enjoyed the bloodshed.

The man lunged in and again stomped on the boy's left foot. This time, the boy was prepared and twisted his body to the right. With all the force he could muster, he delivered an uppercut so fierce that the man was lifted off his feet and fell flat on his back. The men in the crowd could not conceal the looks of worry on their faces as the boy jumped on top of the man and began raining down thunderous fists of his own.

The crowd coerced the referee to jump in, and after a moment of hesitation, he did just that. He pulled the boy off the man and helped him up, eliciting boos from the blacks in the crowd. When both fighters were on their feet and separated, the boy growled and said something even he didn't understand, as he looked at the man who swayed slightly and stood on weary stilts. His will to stand was stronger than his legs, and he stumbled toward the boy and swung wildly from ten feet away. The boy met him again in the center of the ring and rotated his body to deliver another booming right hand to the man.

A filthy man in the crowd had been clutching his pistol at his side since the boy's first punch connected. He scowled at the boy, raised it in the air, and fired. The eruption caused the spectators to scatter. Those who had fallen were trampled, while others fired off their own weapons, their maniacal laughs trailing the sounds of the gunshots. The fight had no winner due to the outburst. The boy's opponent lay flat on his back until his companions came back to help him. The boy stumbled his way back to Walter's home, and the night passed without further incident.

The next morning, the boy pulled open the large wooden doors to Walter's humble blacksmith shop. Walter went to a Mr. John Dutton's home to pay him to accompany him to his wife's plantation, Mr. Dutton being white. The boy opened and closed his mouth, his jaw still in pain from the punches the night before. Though his head was ringing, he began his work. Fifteen minutes later, he stood in front of a burning furnace with sweat forming on his skin. With metal tongs, he grabbed a glowing orange piece of iron from the fire and carefully set it on an anvil. He began to bang away at it with a hammer, altering its shape with each blow. Between strikes, a ruckus came from outside. At first he ignored it, but the racket demanded his attention. He set down the iron and hammer and went over to a drawer. He pulled out his small pistol, placed it in his waistband, and walked over to the large doorway. He cautiously stuck his head out.

A large flock of people waltzed their way down the dirt road, which had been made a mess by the previous week's rainstorms.

So many voices were heard that the group sounded to be talking in some ancient language, the speakers of which were all long deceased. Riding on a team of well-built mules were a group of fearsome-looking men, each with pipes in their mouths, their faces barely visible under their hats. The man the boy fought the night before was among them, and his eyes remained anchored on the boy the entire way. Alongside these men, on foot, ran many other men, women, and even children. A young man placed his arm around another in brotherly fashion as they looked at and spoke to the men on mules. Several children, no older than nine years old, skipped and danced beside the feet of the animals. All had looks of joy on their faces, as though they were taking part in a parade.

Foremost among all these, in fact about five feet in front, rode a man who would have been out of place anywhere else. He had been speaking to a giant of a man who walked nearest to him, and this still being five feet away. His purple linen shirt was open almost down to his navel and flowed gently in the wind. His horse, pristine and elegant, towered above the mules of the men behind him. With heavily feathered legs, the dark-gray horse carefully tiptoed and avoided splashing in any puddles. The leader brought his massive horse up alongside where the boy stood and cast a large shadow over him. He dramatically flung his left leg over the animal, jumped from the mount, and landed with great flare.

The boy looked slightly up at the man, who appeared to be in his forties. A gold chain sat on his sturdy chest. He stared at the boy with pale-blue eyes that looked to be on fire, with an intensity that the boy had never seen before. His handsome, trustworthy face was stretched into a permanent smile that made him look perfectly harmless, though this couldn't be any further from the truth. He dusted his hands off onto his tan pants and stuck out a large, bony hand for the boy to shake.

The nervous boy reached his hand out to meet the man's.

"My name is Argan Zebulon, affectionately known to most as General Zebulon."

With reservation, the boy gave his name.

"Well, it is quite a pleasure to meet you. May the two of us go inside and chat for a spell? It's of a most important matter . . . Ah, yes, pay no mind to these men, for they mean no harm."

The boy stared at the group who watched him. Two black men tipped their hats to the boy and smiled at him, which comforted him for a moment.

Once inside the shop, the General removed his hat and shook his head, letting his sandy-brown hair swing each way. He appeared to take great interest in the shop and everything in it. He picked up and examined a horseshoe that the boy had finished the day before. With childlike curiosity, he held it up to the light that beamed in from a window. To untrained eyes, the shop was a mess, with lanterns never more than ten feet from each other. Buckets and tools of every size and make were strewn everywhere. However, the boy and Walter knew just where everything was placed and liked it that way. The General grabbed a wooden stool and dusted it off before he sat upright and placed the hat on his thighs. The boy grabbed a stool himself and sat about ten feet from the General who spoke first.

"I will get right to it, as I am a busy man. The entire town knows of your battle last night. I, for one, am most impressed. Roger, the gentleman you fought, is possibly one of my strongest men. I myself am not a man of violence and was not present, but when I heard that he had been bested, I had to come meet the man responsible."

The boy's heart was pounding so hard that he was sure it could be seen thumping through his shirt and apron. Even as a child, he very well knew the consequences of roughing up a white man. He was naive in believing that things were different west of the Mississippi. Either that, or he was too drunk to care at the time. Up to his fight with Roger, he had been made to fight other blacks and a few Natives. General Zebulon spoke again.

"How old are you?"

"I turned fifteen not long ago."

"Ahh, what an age, on the brink of manhood. And are you free?"

"Yes, sir."

General Zebulon stood up and dusted off a table before he placed his hat on it. He dramatically cuffed his hands behind his back while he walked to the window and looked out of it. The view was less than stellar, and he glared at the side of a watchmaker's shop next door.

"Fifteen years old and free, with so much life and promise ahead of you, yet so many man-made barriers to impede that progress. Just what is it that you want out of life?" the General asked.

The boy thought and remembered when his parents had asked him a similar question. He didn't have a straight answer then, and he didn't have one now.

"Well, I've always had the urge to travel. Leave my problems behind and just go. I want to really be my own man and live how I want to live. My happiness is somewhere out there, and I just need to find it."

"Beautiful slogans . . . Is that all?" The General turned back toward the boy and did not seem satisfied with that answer.

"I guess I want to know what it's like to not have to answer to any white man."

General Zebulon now gave a large smile, showing his perfect teeth.

"Well, son, as providence might have it, I know of such a place where all your wants and more can become reality, if you will it to be so. Where you can feel the full extent of God's heavenly promise, whether you be white, green, pink, or Negro!"

Zebulon now had the boy's complete interest. The boy unconsciously raised an eyebrow while he moved toward the edge of his stool. The General flamboyantly pointed his arms to the direction he assumed to be west.

"To our west, some one hundred miles, sits God's country. Where the only laws to be followed are His and His alone. Laws that even the half-naked, heathen savages who worship false idols would not dare deny. A country where you answer to no white man, without him understanding the law of retaliation. Your urge to travel will be satisfied, as you would be among a select few of not just Negro men but men in general to lay eyes on a country so beautiful, it may bring you to tears. With mountains that make a man feel his insignificance in the world, even if he were the king of many nations. Where untouched rivers wind through prairies so wide that they themselves resemble the ocean that your ancestors and mine came across, of course under different circumstances. Where all your problems are tossed into the wind and carried away to land on the back of some other man. How does all of this sound to you?"

"Like you're answering my dreams," the boy said. A large tear formed in his eye.

"How aware are you with the fur trade?"

"You mean like beavers? Not much."

"Precisely beavers. To give you the short of it, the fur of those small creatures can be sold for as much as six dollars a pound back east. We find them, trap them, skin them, and get rich in the process. It's that simple!"

"And you're proposing that I join you?"

"Ambitious and intelligent," he said, smiling. "I am looking for men such as yourself to join me in the mountains. Men who not only want more out of life but have the desire to do something about it."

"But I'm only fifteen."

"Minor details. Many young boys your age have seized control of their lives and raced into the mountains. I have just formed the Far West Fur Company, quite an enterprising venture! I would be honored to have you as a part of my . . . our, first journey into God's country, where man and beast alike roam free."

"Mister Zebulon, I . . ."

"Please, call me General Zebulon."

"General Zebulon, I don't know if you noticed, but Negroes ain't never been too well liked. If white folks attack and assault us in civilized society, why would it be any different where there ain't any rules? And what about the man from last night?"

The General's face quickly turned very serious. Unlike the rest of his speech, this was too real to have been rehearsed.

"Son, as the Almighty God watches over us, you have my word that no man shall molest you based on your race. If he does, I will raise his hair off him myself and gift it to you as a souvenir."

"You'll do what?"

"Raise his hair. Scalp him."

"Does that happen often?"

The boy envisioned some faceless Native seizing a fistful of hair and running his blade through it. He cringed at the idea.

"Not much. A few men have been, but it is a rare occurrence. It is practiced by savages mostly." The General smiled again. "So, what do you say? Will you make history with me? Will you chase after your happiness? Or will you continue to drink your life away? Fighting in circles like some gamecock until a mob of white men drags you away for you to never be seen again?"

The boy looked at the hammer he had been using earlier. He stared at the anvil and pictured himself banging away at it thirty years in the future. He asked himself if he would be happy. The large double doors were closed, but he gazed at them, and thoughts raced through his mind with all that awaited him in "God's country." His earlier thought of being scalped was gone. It had been replaced with half-witted fantasies. He pictured meeting half-naked Natives with long braided hair as they taught him how to use a bow and arrow. He saw himself running after beaver and shooting the fat bastards for target practice. He visualized himself sleeping under the stars on a green lush blanket of grass, while a gentle night breeze swept over him. Most importantly, he saw himself not having to produce his freedom papers to any man. For the first time since he had been in New Orleans, his face transposed into something of a half-smile. The air of God's country would clear his mind or, at the very least, provide another distraction.

"I'm in," he said.

The General strolled over to him, made him stand up, and opened his arms wide. The hug itself surprised the boy, and the strength of it shocked him even further. With a baffled look on his face, he attempted to push the General away. Who was this strange man before him, who found himself comfortable enough to hug a black man? He was flashy and flamboyant for sure, and seemed to live in a world owned by himself and governed by himself, where other humans played a part in the role he assigned them. The General was already an interesting man, but most of all he appeared to be free. Free from the opinions of others, free from stress, and at perfect peace with himself. These naive notions appealed to the boy's young mind. The General took a step back.

"I knew you would."

The General went over to the doors of the shop and thrust them open with great showmanship. He was greeted by the stares of the townspeople that seemed to have gone from jubilation to impatience. This, the General did not seem to either notice or care.

"Good people of St. Louis, return to your homes and rejoice at the continuance of life that you have been privileged to see. The young man who you have expected to see harmed has now found employment with the Far West Fur Company!"

Chants of "Aw, hell" and more were yelled by many of the people. A young boy of about eight stomped in the dirt and stormed away. The crowd returned to where they had come from, cursing and muttering all along. The General stared at Roger, who looked to have only somewhat recovered from the previous night.

"Roger, the young man has expressed a concern about any form of retaliation on your part. If you would fancy another go at him, please do so now."

Roger dismounted his mule and moved gingerly toward the boy. He turned his head and spat before he reached out his hand to shake the boy's.

"I can take a whippin,' Zebulon. I seen too many summers to be fightin,' anyway, so don't you worry about that. Out there? I feel safer with this one on our side."

The General gave an elated smile. He called to a British-born man named Charles. He, too, dismounted and came over to the two men and stared at them through one eye, the other covered by a patch.

"Sign up our newest member!" he said to the cyclops.

Preparation for the journey took up the next few days. The morning of their departure, the boy left a note for Walter, who still slept. With the first pink light beginning to show, the boy walked as he had when he left his home. Tall and upright, as straight as an arrow. He awkwardly bounced to the expedition's camp, which was on a small hill about a half mile from the Mississippi.

His confidence wavered as he walked past men. They were young and old, and sharpened knives with edges so razor-like that they could cut just by looking at them. They cleaned three-foot-long .50 caliber Hawken rifles that were made by the two famous brothers in this town.

A line of mules stood and fought with the men who placed packs on them. The supplies contained flint, gunpowder, balls of lead, hatchets, beaver traps, wool and buffalo-skin blankets, Mexican-made saddles, and skinning knives.

The boy found the General who gave him a warm greeting. He was introduced to a young American man named James Calloway. James helped him gather his provisions and place them on the mules.

"I'm from the backwoods of Virginny. No, sir, ain't no love for no man in them woods. Only the strongest come out of there," he said.

He looked up at the boy, who towered over him, and when they shook hands, the boy noticed that James squeezed his hand extra tight. His mustache revealed him to be somewhat older than the boy. He spoke again after he looked at the boy's boots.

"Yes, sir," started James. "These here boots? I walked all the way from Virginny to St. Louis in these here boots, and they seen every bit of hardship that I have. Where from, friend?"

"Tennessee," the boy said.

"I come across quite a heap of trouble coming through them forests there. A whole family of black bears chased after me. They woulda ate me had I not shot the mama in her neck . . . This yer first time goin' out west?"

"Yea. I'm a little nervous, are you? I hear them Indins are cruel out there."

"Hell no! I can whoop any Indin west of the Mississippi, and that's for fact!"

The boy thought that James talked too much and was too boastful, but he liked him. He listened intently to James's outlandish stories and hadn't noticed the multitude of people that joined to send off the expedition. It looked as if the entire city showed up, as families and friends cried tears of sorrow and joy. Wives kissed their husbands, afraid to never see them again. In some cases, this was true. Daughters gripped their fathers' legs and held onto ribbons from their hair that were gifted for good luck, while some of the men without family members present shed silent tears and wished for a speedy exit. The command was given to shoot off muskets as the expedition began its trek up the Mississippi River, where they expected to meet the Missouri River in about fifteen miles. A line of more than twenty-five men, armed with more than fifty mules, walked off. The population watched the almost weekly ritual until they were out of sight. The boy walked, leading his two pack mules and looked back to James.

"Where are the rest of our horses?" he asked as they both looked up toward the front of the line. General Zebulon sat tall on his horse, his face welcoming the warmth of that early morning sun.

5

Deadly Encounters

T he boy marched in the middle of the pack train with James and a young Frenchman named Jacques. Jacques spoke little to no English and understood few words that were over a syllable in length. Jacques would often nod and smile whenever he saw the boy doing so, as James bragged on and on about himself. The group reached the point where the Missouri River met the Mighty Mississippi. They began their westward ascent along the south bank of the river.

Some miles down it, on the opposite bank, sat the village of St. Charles. Massive, one-hundred-foot sycamore trees partially hid the quiet settlement. Like most frontier towns, there was not much to see. What they could see were large American-made homes built along a single brick-laid street. They went on and came to the town of La Charrette, which grew around the old French fort of the same name. The quiet trading post sat atop a hill that gave a two-hundred-foot bird's-eye view of the river. There they encountered many groups much like themselves, rough and hard looking. Men representing every race and nationality. Small, dark men from West African nations, gruff Europeans, a Mexican or two, all convened in one place.

They passed the small trading post of Jefferson City and came to a wide-open prairie. Small homesteads dotted the sparsely populated region. They purchased corn from the French inhabitants and continued on.

The men passed the community of Lexington, a town looking much like all those previously described. A few miles from the community they came across various rundown plantations. The General gave a sympathetic eye to the destitute-looking blacks in the tobacco fields. He made the sign of the cross and bowed his head to them before they marched on.

By now, each day had become increasingly similar to the one before it. They would wake before sunrise and eat their breakfast. They would need the strength to begin the fights with their old mules, who often tossed their packs off them. At noon they ate a quick lunch and allowed the animals to rest and graze. After about an hour, the monotonous march continued until after sunset, when the call of "catch up" went out. The men would buzz around their site like ants and pitched tents on each corner of a hollow square, with one side of it being open to the river. One-foot-long stakes were driven into the middle of the square, with the purpose of securing the mules. When this was done, they began dinner, which was nothing more than boiled corn when hunting missions were not successful. They told stories, smoked, and joked around until eight o'clock, when the men went to sleep, leaving a few men on night guard to rotate shifts. In the morning, they woke and repeated the process with little variation, day after day, night after night.

One night in particular, the boy reclined on his buffalo robe and smoked a pipe. The smoke hurt his lungs the first few puffs, but after about a week, he got used to it and how to smoke it. He stared at an old man named Henry, who sat at the edge of the campfire, his dark face glowing from the light. His boisterous voice grabbed ahold of most of the group's attention. His demonstrative gestures seized whatever was left of it. Zebulon sat with his legs crossed and his eyes closed. His body swayed slightly, and he looked to be in a trance as he listened to the man with a smile on his face.

The sight of a man to the boy's left caught his attention. He crouched at the edge of the fire and held a mirror. He shaved his head, which already was little more than peach fuzz. His face lacked wrinkles, and he didn't look to be much older than twenty-five.

"He's a strange one, ain't he?"

The boy looked over to the speaker. His name was Bradan, and his Irish accent could not be ignored.

"What's he doing?" the boy asked.

"He scared stiff of them Indins raisin' his hair, so he cuts it all off. That's me younger brother, Sammy. Everyone calls him 'Sammy No Scalp.'"

The boy sat quiet for a moment.

"That makes a lot of sense, actually," he said. Sammy finished and now was bald as a stone. He tied a bandanna over his dome, walked over, and sat on the robe next to his brother.

"What you scared of them Indins for?" the boy asked. "If you don't mess with them, they don't mess with you, right?"

"Ain't no tellin' when it comes to a savage," Bradan said.

"If you don't give them Indins no hair to raise, you just gone make them mad," said an old black man named Roy. He leisurely leaned back on his elbows.

"You rather lose some hair or yer neck?" asked James.

Sammy opened his mouth to speak, but Bradan cut him off.
"He ain't losin' neither. They have to go through me first."

"I'll whoop every Indin we come across," said James. He looked over toward the few half-French, half-Native men that rode with them. "I mean no offense. I'm talkin' about them Indins that run around in cloth."

The next morning, the boy received his first taste of life in "God's country." The group was busy packing up the mules. They gave every man trouble except for one; the giant who never left the General's side. He stood over six and a half feet tall and weighed upward of three hundred pounds. His mules almost eagerly accepted their packs without any incident. His massive hands rubbed their long heads, and he often kissed the animals, touching his scraggly beard against their faces.

While he stood in tranquility with the mules, on the other side of camp, Roger struggled with one of his that he had named Hard Time. He pulled her, and she firmly rooted her front legs into the ground and stretched her neck out. Each time he pulled, she put up more of an effort to remain were she stood. Roger cursed and spat, calling the mule every foul word he had ever heard.

James walked over and in his attempt to assist Roger, he received a soft kick to his stomach almost as a warning. The General sat high on his horse and supervised the entire episode. His face had gone from delight to nonchalance to anger. He dismounted his horse and walked over to the mule. He spoke softly to the mule and rubbed her head in a circular pattern. When he grabbed the reins and attempted to lead her, she again drove her feet into the ground and would not be moved. He glared at her, pulled out his pistol, and fired at point-blank range. Hard Time's lifeless body fell over on her side as stiff as a log.

"It's quite a shame, but time is of the essence. There's much to see!" the General said with a smile as he mounted his horse and gave the order to ride out. The boy stared at the General with reverence before he helped Roger and James place the packs onto one of the spare mules, and the men proceeded west.

Around noon, they came to fifteen-foot walls that surrounded the abandoned Fort Osage. Inside the walls sat the eerie remnants of a factory, officers' quarters, soldiers' huts, and a stockade. A few hundred yards from the fort sat a village of Osage Natives. They often traded with companies that used this trail on the road to Santa Fe. Men, women, and children came out, eager to meet the company. In their arms were dried animal skins, knives, food, bows, and hatchets, just to name a few. The men carried dried animal skins, knives, food, bows, hatchets, and other articles. The boy made a mental note of the height of the Osage men, who on average were over six feet tall with most of the company having to look up at them.

From afar, the boy watched the Osage chief. Tall and robust like the rest of his people, he looked the General eye to eye as they spoke. His beautifully made white-and-blue robe bounced with each hand sign, as the two spoke in a blend of signals and broken English.

Standing next to the General was the large man that the entire company had been told to call Grunt. His protective, intimidating air hovered over the General. He was without a doubt ready to spring into action should the Osage show one false move. While the Osage chief had a welcoming air about him, the General's discomfort became more apparent. His face was frozen in a forced, uneasy smile, and his arms folded tight across his body.

"Zebulon don't look too happy right now, do he?" the boy asked James.

"Only around them Indins."

When the chief appeared to be done talking, the General called for a gray mule in particular. Grunt brought the animal over to him and relieved it of a barrel that was attached to a rope, hanging over its side. Grunt gathered at a fire pit and with a flint and steel and started a large blaze that was contained in a fire pit. The General grabbed a cup, dipped it into the spout of the barrel, and held it up to measure carefully. He tossed the whiskey and when it splashed onto the fire, a large fireball shot high up toward the sky, as did a cheer from all the Osage. The chief smiled and shook the General's hand while the General smirked devilishly.

The next morning they resumed their westward course. Many of the Osage men were fast asleep due to the previous night's alcoholic revelry. The company looked over at the Osage village as women watched and waved farewells to them. About one hundred oblong, wooden lodges were covered in leaves. A group of children made use of the twenty feet that separated each lodge. They danced and laughed in blissful ignorance of the dire situation their culture was in. A woman placed several scalps on poles atop the chief's lodge in preparation for the dance that night. She waved to the men and continued to arrange the bloody trophies. The boy shuddered at the sight, and they moved on.

Pass the fort, the country continued in monotony. They reached the mouth of the Kansas River without incident. One morning, the General crouched down by the river and tossed dark-brown water on his face. Surrounding him were Sammy,

Old Roy, and Bradan.

"We not gonna make it on the backs of them mules," Roy said.

"Nonsense! I feel fine and spirited. We are progressing according to schedule."

"Before long, everything you see before you will be covered in snow up to your kneecap and we gonna be stuck right in the middle of it if we can't move quicker."

The General looked over at the rest of the group. Roger's facial expression showed that he agreed with Roy.

"We need those horses," Sammy said.

"What say you, Bill?"

A large middle-aged man stepped forward for his chance to speak. Sweat glistened off his balding head. The sun had baked his skin for many summers now, as he had more experience than any other man in the wilderness.

"I 'ssumed that the goal was to always acquire some horses. Ain't too many men crossed them prairies without 'em."

The General ran the silty water through his hair. He styled it to his liking before he stood and walked over to his horse while the group waited patiently. His walk looked to have been somewhat uncomfortable, as if each step were carefully thought of. Even the way he held his shoulders appeared to be calculated, almost like a part of some act, the boy thought. He quickly tossed the thought as foolishness. After all, the free nature of the General was the reason he agreed to come to the West. Men like the General existed, and they were fearless. They said what they meant, were true to themselves, and most of all, they were free. Any thought against these notions would mean the boy was wrong. If he were wrong, that would mean that he himself could never be the fearless man he desired to be.

The General returned with a piece of large canvas rolled up in his hand. He flapped it open and held it up for himself and Bill to see.

"We happen to be close to a village of the Kaw," he said.

"They just lost a whole heap of land to the government, so I dunno how friendly they gonna be to whites," Bill replied.

"Hmm. Fear not, Bill, for I am a forward thinker. In that case, we shall send our Negro counterparts." He called over to the boy, Roy, and James. "Apparently everyone is in need of horses," he joked. "I am trusting you men to go with Bill and purchase seventy-five horses from the sava— the Kaw, and herd them back to us."

They all agreed and immediately set off for the village of the Kaw Natives. They marched through a picturesque countryside. Trees with beautiful orange, yellow, and red leaves covered the rolling landscape. The boy felt peaceful out there and at times would close his eyes and feel the region's fall climate surround him. For some time, they did not pass a soul that did not flap wings or walk on four legs. The boy had taken a spoke to Roy.

"You know the scariest thing about being out in the woods, Roy?"

"What's that?"

"It's a hell of a lot more that see us than we see them."

As he said this, a black bear stood motionless and watched the group walk by, undetected.

They made camp for the night near the river, and minutes later, the boy stared down the length of his rifle. In his sights was a young deer from about two hundred feet away. It innocently grazed from the lush river valley as Old Roy whispered tips to the boy.

"Hold your breath and feel your heartbeat. In between beats, you take your shot. Not a second before or a second after."

The boy calmed himself and did just that. When the smoke rolled away from his sight, the deer lay on the ground. Its strong body twitched as it attempted to rise. The boy jumped and skipped his way over to the carcass, pulled out his knife, and immediately slit its throat.

There was once a time when he could not kill a chicken without crying in a corner, but those days were long gone. Almost as if he were becoming desensitized to murder in general. This thought darted through his mind before he passed it off as unwarranted. The group celebrated his kill and enjoyed a chilly night on a plush blanket of earth.

The next morning, they began to grumble about whether the Kaw village actually existed. James and the boy turned to Roy, who deferred to Bill. With unsure eyes, he assured them that the village was "more close than far." After two more hours in the wilderness, they came to an area that had been cleared of all trees. A well-built brick home sat at the center of the clearing. It was rare to see an American-made home this far from so-called civilization. The men jumped at the thought of seeing an American face.

"That Kaw village ain't look to be too far. I'll go ask the man for directions," said Bill.

At the back of the house sat a small garden with an even smaller yield of corn growing. Chickens bobbed around the rows of corn and continuously pecked at the ground. About one hundred yards from the home sat a pen full of strong-looking horses. Horses were highly prized possessions in this land, and it was strange that they were so far from the home. The group came up to the front door with Bill at the helm. He gave the door a gentle knock and spoke.

"We need directions. We bring no trouble and are white." He pulled James up in front of Roy and the boy.

After a few moments, a small brown woman opened the wooden door and peered through the crack. When she saw that they were Americans, she relaxed her round face and smiled. A half-blooded child hid behind her, clutching onto her left leg. He began to whimper when he looked up into Bill's small, beady eyes.

Through signs and broken English, they were able to ascertain that her husband was a white man. He set up a trading post back toward the east and was not home. The woman was a daughter of the Kaw village and informed them that it was not too far. At times as she spoke, Bill did not seem to have paid much attention to what she attempted to say. Her long, raven-colored hair and beautiful young face could captivate a blind man. Bill stared at her with those terrible eyes. The boy thought nothing of this as they thanked her and kept marching.

A few miles later, they saw in the distance one hundred or so small oval huts about five feet high. Each was covered with dried buffalo and deer skins. Willow branches and leaves were plastered onto the thatched roofs. Women tended to large cornfields that cast a large lake of yellow in the background. The Kaw gave them a warm welcome, and the chief treated them with the utmost respect.

His name was translated to mean Dark Cloud, and he stood head and shoulder above the majority of the Kaw men. He had large, wide eyes that appeared to forever be passing judgement. Bill spoke to him in signs and made a gesture toward a large cache of horses, about half a mile in the distance. The chief smiled and readily sold them seventy-five horses from their stock, and he sent them away with kind words.

The group traveled back toward the east and again came past the home of the Kaw woman and camped not far from it. At night, Roy and James were the first on watch duty and around midnight, they woke the boy and Bill for their turn. The boy threw an internal fight each time they woke him. This was his least-favorite duty, next to cooking the meat. Under the cover of night, he wasn't sure that he could even shoot the ground in front of him, let alone an enemy.

In the moonlight, the herd looked to be statues, sleeping in a strange manner. An occasional gust of wind caught the boy's attention but other than this, all was quiet and ideal. The boy watched over them and began to grow bored. He rode over to Bill.

"Say, Bill, what's the difference in them Indins and, say, the Cherokee?"

"Not a goddamn thing. No matter where you find 'em, they'll be half naked, backward, and savage. Don't matter if it's them Ree, Blackfeet, Shianne, don't matter, they all the same. They only love whiskey and horses. You come arrive with both, and they almost make you chief."

The boy felt nervous and, without meaning to, gave a fake laugh.

"You know," Bill continued, "kind of like niggers."

The boy's heart skipped a beat, and he did not know what to say. He half thought of waking up Roy, who definitely knew how to handle this situation. But Bill would only scold him for not handling his own problems, and he decided against it. Bill had always made the boy feel uneasy. The man always attempted to have some sort of camaraderie with the boy, who did not trust him at all. Bill's blue eyes were like a viper's, piercing and shifty. They made the boy uncomfortable each time he looked into them. Once Bill saw that the boy would not reply, he spoke again.

"No matter what I've seen in this life, I never seen a nigger do any good for anyone, anywhere. The only thing lower than an Indin would be a nigger, and that ain't too far behind."

He looked over at the boy, who sat stunned. His mouth refused to move, and his hands began to sweat. He searched his flustered mind for the appropriate words to reject this notion.

"Not you, though," Bill said. "You one of the good ones, I can always tell."

About an hour later, Bill rode back over to the boy.

"You go ahead and get some sleep."

"What about the horses?" the boy said.

"They'll be fine. All's mighty quiet, ain't a livin' thing moving."

"You sure?"

"Yea, I'll watch it."

The boy was excited to get back to sleep, and by noon of the following day, they returned to the rest of the group and were met with applause. The herd of fresh, robust-looking horses high-stepped their way into camp. The boy chose a beautiful, chestnut-colored horse of Arabian stock that he named Socrates. It held a strong, spirited look in its eyes and quickly took to liking the boy and the boy to it.

That night, a cool breeze swept over the men. After eating, the men sat around the fire and joked.

"If we hadn't got them horses, I dunno if Old Roy's hooves would have held out another week," joked James.

Roy looked perplexed before he spoke.

"The good Lord broke the mold when He stitched me together.

I could be run over by an oxcart and still be of greater leg than a young'un like you," he shot back.

Zebulon smiled and interjected.

"Have you always spoken to whites in this manner?"

"You bet your hind I did, even worse when I was the pup's age." He looked at the boy, referring to him. "I was somethin' to see," he said as he closed his eyes and drifted away. His body was lying on his robe, but his mind was now gliding through time and space.

"While I'm certainly glad they haven't, I'm surprised you were never strung up in someone's tree," the General retorted.

Here, Henry stood and addressed the audience.

"It has appeared to me that you gentlemen are not fully aware of who you are privileged to share a campfire with! The same fire that warms each and every one of you also warms not only an esteemed member of the Negro race but all humans. Picture this!" He waved his hands through the air and cupped them as if he could indeed grab ahold of it.

"God damnit, Henry! I don't wanna hear that Negro shit tonight!" yelled a hunter from Kentucky named Kenneth Brown.

"Ah, Ken, even you will find strength and inspiration from this tale. Now, ahh yes, picture this. At the time our story began, our hero had walked this earth for no more than fifteen years and every day for each of those years he had been forced to work against his will AND the will of God for the wealth and comfort of a cruel master. Our hero was known throughout the entire county as being of 'great leg' and was quicker than any man and several beasts, so when he was called upon to deliver a message, it was of no surprise. Well, he found himself lost in a forest so thick that the sun's rays decided to not reach the forest floor, turning day into dusk, allowing him to see no more than twenty feet in front of him. He hears sounds that could only come from countless beasts of unexplainable origins, and when he looks up, he stares into the faces of not one but two large black bears! Their small dark eyes stared into his soul. Teeth sharper than knives showed when they began to smile at him like little devils. The dark and sinister gazes would have pierced and shaken any man to his core, but even as a boy, our hero was far from being run of the mill. He came from men that survived the storms, hunger, ungodly diseases, and brutal treatment that came with crossing that unforgiving ocean from Africa to this nation. The foul beasts smelled the fear oozing from his pores and sprung at him in an instant. One weighing five hundred pounds, with claws as long as a scalping knife. Our hero narrowly escapes the swipe and retreats up a tree but, poor fool! Not knowing that these bears, too, climb trees, they gave chase and one of the monsters took a swipe at his right leg and ripped a chunk of his flesh off. They sat below him eating of it as if it were covered in the sweetest honey."

Henry's method of storytelling was unparalleled. Each man watched him and did not allow their minds to drift from the topic at hand. The firelight showed the glistening sweat that came from his forehead. He moved around, jumped, and screamed as he related the tale. Two hours prior, Henry's movements were slow and stiff. Now in his element, he moved like a man more than half his age. He channeled the characters and portrayed their emotions onto his audience. He continued speaking.

"Our hero was now stuck in a tree with these thirsty monsters below him, laughing and hungry for more of his flesh, but this story would not be told had he not shown his legendary status.

He grabbed a knife off his waistband, and with all the might he could muster tossed it at the chest of one of the scoundrels. It hit it dead center in the heart, and struck it dead instantly! The larger bear lamented over the death of its evil friend, giving our hero time to come up with a plan.

"He stared for a few seconds and decided that the best plan was to not plan! For a man can adapt to any situation he is placed in, and without any further thought, he dropped from the tree and landed on the back of the snare, and with his great arms, our hero wrapped around the bear's neck and cut all air to its lungs. The beast struggled and growled, scratched and clawed. Its long nails sunk deep into his forearms, and he nearly gave up, but no beast can break the will of man! The creature fell to its side and on its back, crushing our young hero under its immense weight but still he held on, knowing that to let go would mean to surrender to death. Only once the bear stopped moving did he release it, having crushed its throat. He struggled to get to one knee but when he did, he stood over the two dead creatures and screamed out like a beast himself!"

James sat with his mouth wide open and for once was speechless. The boy unconsciously smiled as he looked over at Roy. The old man pulled up his pants leg to reveal a scar where someone or something had indeed ripped a chunk of his leg out.

"That true, Roy?" he asked.

As if the scar was not enough, Roy grabbed a necklace from under his shirt and showed a large bear tooth, and then he spoke.

"You heard him? The words out of his mouth are all ordered by the Lord. I told ye. It would take three of ye to whoop me now and seven back then!"

All that night, the boy wondered if he were "man enough" to kill even one bear. He hoped to come across one and prove himself. If Roy could do it at the same age, the boy was capable as well.

It was now late October, and the chill of the nights gave way to welcomed warmth from the early-morning sun. The group hummed around, each engaged in their respective duties. Sammy and Bradan fetched water from the river. They would place it next to other jars that had inch-thick layers of sediment on the bottom.

The General sat up high on his horse and watched over the morning's operations. Roy volunteered the boy to ride and watch over the company's horses as they grazed. Socrates had its own head down to the grass. The boy rubbed his neck and looked up to a wonderful view of the fall colors that remained on a set of trees off to his right. He spoke to himself.

"I guess this really is 'God's country.'" The boy could see his breath twirl away in the early-morning chill. "But wasn't back home once 'God's country,' too? So if they keep movin' west, will God's country keep movin' also? Or does somethin' out here make this more special?"

He interrupted himself when off to his left, about a mile away, movement caught his attention. Faint outlines moved toward him. Soon the bodies of men mounted on horses, much like their herd, became visible. Their robes trailed in the wind as the horses sped across the ground at a furious pace. Each man was armed with lances that were five feet in length, bows with arrows so sharp that they looked to be able to pierce a rock, and secondhand muskets from French traders that were more useful as melee objects. A terrible-looking band of warriors, with dark-red paint garnished on their open chests and faces that gave them demonic appearances.

"Ho," the boy yelled out to Roy. "Them look like Indins to you?"

Roy rode over to the boy and took a long, hard look at the horde of men that charged toward them.

"I'd say so."

Zebulon rode over to the two of them as they now had the attention of the entire party.

The ever-present smile on his face grew dim and was now replaced with a look of concern. His eyes grew cold and lost their typical fire. He looked altogether like a different man.

"Round the horses," he said.

They gathered some of the horses, herded them nearer to the camp, and waited. The boy slung his rifle from his back and held onto it. His hands shook as he watched the mob come toward them. He counted twenty, fifty, no seventy-five of them all riding in their direction. When they were one hundred yards out, they stopped. Well over one hundred strong, stoic-looking men stared at the company. Their eyes were full of anger and vengeance. The Kaw chief, Dark Cloud, sat ten feet in front of his men and made no signs of peace toward them. The boy spoke out once he recognized Dark Cloud. On his left was the woman from the home they stopped at. Her eyes were cold and piercing.

"Hold! That's Dark Cloud, the Kaw chief that sold us them horses. They'll treat us well," he yelled out.

The boy thought that they were here to warn the company of some danger ahead. A shrill war whoop echoed throughout the area and pierced away all hope of a friendly meeting. The assailants raised their bows and dispatched a volley of arrow shafts that plunged down to the earth, narrowly missing the boy. He lost his balance on the horse as it jumped and screamed. He looked up from the ground as a pack of revenge-laden men sped toward the company, all making the sound of that soul-shattering shriek.

6

The General's Folly

The General was a flamboyant man without shame. This shined through every aspect of his lifestyle. Prone to outbursts of tears and laughter, one sometimes bringing forth the other. He was quick to wrap his arms around anyone at any time. As a youth, his peers often described him as "queer and effeminate." Those same men would now shed tears of joy had they seen his cool head during battle. He did not flinch once as arrows and lead balls zipped past him. He rode over to the boy and blocked any arrows from hitting him while he fired his rifle. He then pulled his horse to a retreat and yelled orders at the tops of his lungs. His men withdrew and set the river at their backs as they formed a defensive line.

Under his direction, a group of undisciplined mavericks moved with military-like efficiency. They readied their rifles and fired at his command. A line of Kaw fell as the black gun smoke rolled along with the course of the river, and the men began to reload. Waves of arrows and lances came crashing around them, some which found their way in shoulders, hands and legs.

In typical fighting custom, the Kaw had formed a line and rushed at the company. It was next to impossible to miss an enemy that fought in this way. Even the most inexperienced shooters appeared to be seasoned veterans in this battle. In this way, many Kaw were knocked off of their horses or had their horses shot from under them. The boy stared through the iron sight at a young warrior. He had survived the first wave of shots and continued to make a valiant charge toward the company. The red paint on the young man's face became clearer as he moved closer, causing the boy to hesitate for a moment. When the boy fired, red blood plastered on his naked chest as he flipped backward off his horse. The boy's hands trembled, and he fumbled with the maple stock of the rifle as he struggled to reload. An arrow zipped by his left side and cut out a small sliver of his flesh.

The Kaw chief held a whistle made out of a quail's bone in his right hand. When he blew, his warriors retreated. Several of their brethren either lay lifeless, or crawled on the makeshift battlefield. The company gave collective shouts of joy and thrust their rifles into the air. They released loud curses to the "savages." None were louder than James, who fired his first and only shot at the retreating enemy.

Seventeen bloodied Kaw bodies dirtied that pristine land-scape. Within seconds, several of the company were already hunched over, collecting their trophies.

"You see, the key is to raise the hair while they still warm," said Roger, with no sympathy in his eyes. "You want in on this, No Scalp?" he smiled. He ran his blade through a thin strip of human hair as though he were shucking a piece of corn.

Scalping the Kaw was a strange task due to the manner in which they wore their hair. Their heads were completely shaven, except for a long braided lock that sat on the top of the head and ran down toward their backs. The lock was ornamented with beautiful bright feathers, spliced up with the hair of some animal and almost always decorated with the bone of some beast.

The boy nervously shook while he stood over a dead foe. The rest of the company surrounded him, taunting him endlessly. Blood filled their eyes, and they looked to be demons eager to watch the "pup" take his first trophy of war. He held the scalping instrument loose in his hand. It was a miracle that his shaking didn't cause it to fall. The sneers of the company increased as they grew more impatient. The boy's shoulders sat up high and tense. It was one thing to kill a man, he thought. But it was another to defile his already dead body. He stood motionless for a second, with a look of uncertainty. In his hesitation, the General walked over to him, looking very much different from his usual self.

His hair was in an untidy mess and his white linen shirt was covered in black powder. There was a tear in the shirt near his elbow, where an arrow had narrowly missed him. Forceful yet somehow still polite, he pushed the boy out of his way. He took his left hand and grasped the lock of hair and coiled the braid around his hand and wrist. He put a foot on the man's chest and with the knife in his right hand, he began to circle the top of the man's head. A small trickle of blood streamed down the Kaw's face and strangely resembled a tear when it reached the man's eye. When the lock was separated, the General handed it over to the boy and addressed the company in a calm, cool voice.

"Now, go get the rest of my horses." He then turned and mounted his horse.

The thick braid of hair dripped blood from the small piece of scalp that was attached to it. One look at it caused James to throw up. The General gave him a cold stare of disappointment. His horse pranced around the arrow shafts, allowing the General to analyze the damage. The men nursed their superficial wounds. None were seriously injured, by Kaw hands at least.

"I'm sorry. Aw, hell," Sammy No Scalp yelled.

He dropped to the side of a man named Carl Jackson. For a man who had been shot, he did not look to be in a bad way. His pale face had become a dark pink, due to the laughing which arose from the pit of his soul. He ran his hand through his messy hair and lay back on the ground. He shut his brown eyes and his chest began to convulse up and down. The General sat up tall on his horse and surveyed the man.

"When were they close enough to shoot you?" he asked.

"Fuck," Sammy yelled while he examined the wound. In his fear, he discharged his rifle by accident and relieved Carl of a small chunk of meat from the back of his leg. Once his laughter died down, Carl spoke.

"It's fine, it's fine. I forgive you. It's funny that in a battle against the Indins, I get shot by my own man!"

The other men were hysterical and berated Sammy for his clumsiness. The General watched all this with a stoic face.

"Let's get moving, men! We gotta put distance between them and us. They'll double back around lookin' for hair, you can bet on that," he said.

Ten minutes later, they were off. A long trail of men, horses, and mules headed north along the river. They peered over their shoulders often, afraid to find a horde of Kaw racing toward them.

That night, the moon sat high in the cloudless sky and

illuminated the entire countryside. The company camped without a fire under a blanket of trees along a high bluff of the river. Each man was anxious and on high alert as Zebulon spoke of the attack.

"What the hell happened when you all purchased them horses?" he asked Bill.

"Nothin' out the ordinary."

The General stared at Bill. The moonlight showed telltale signs of dishonesty. His jaw was tightly clenched. Sweat poured down his balding head until he wiped it with a kerchief and continued to speak.

"I dunno nothin' about that. You can't reason with a savage. You've said so yourself, Argan."

"Somethin' ain't weighin' right," said Roger.

"They savages! Hungry for white blood. Ain't much figuring for you to do. W-what else ya need to know? We come through tramplin' on they land, and they never not once was happy with it," said Bill.

"If they wanted to kill, they would've done so while you were at their village. It's almost as if they realized something happened after the fact," said the General.

"Godless, heathen bastards, Argan. No more, no less."

"Yes, but for the time being, we are in their land. It's best to make friends of the Indian."

"I dunno but if they come back, we'll give it to 'em again."

Bill leisurely blew smoke into the air and was finished with the matter. The General was still not satisfied with that answer. He and Bill had known each other for two years now, and he could tell when something was amiss, so he pressed on.

"A young woman sat next to the chief while they attacked. Even for a savage, that is most unusual. Would she happen to have had anything to do with it?"

The boy perked up, wondering what this meant. Bill said nothing, but the energy among the group said it all.

"Bill . . . Tell me you didn't."

"I . . ."

"Oh God," the General exalted. He stood up and scurried his hands through his hair. He wandered away from the group and muttered to himself. He was gone for about thirty seconds before his faint outline returned. He gave Bill a blank stare and walked over to him. About two feet from him, Zebulon pulled out his pistol and cocked the hammer. His hand shook feverishly and the pistol rattled. No one moved and all the men watched, eager to see the next move.

"Argan, you ain't gonna shoot . . ."

Though the company watched and anticipated the shooting, the loud bang made everyone jump. Bill fell on his side and wailed in pain. He held onto his groin as the rest of the men recovered from the initial shock and sat back silent, with wide eyes. Even in the dark, the boy thought that he could see fire in Zebulon's eyes. He remembered back to when he first met the General in St. Louis and how warm and inviting he had been. The boy did not know many killers, but when he woke up that morning, he was sure that the General was not one. This was the same man who kept his fingernails clean and trim. He often complained about dirt on his clothes. It was strange to see that he was responsible for what the boy estimated to be at least three dead Kaw. And now no remorse was in the General's eyes, and even less was in his voice as he hissed.

"That is one thing you do NOT do, even to a savage." Had the moonlight not hit the tear in his eye just right, it never would have been seen. He appeared to have taken the act as personal, or perhaps it evoked some memory in him. "Grunt, hog-tie him."

Grunt made a low-pitched noise in confirmation and stood. Like a mindless beast, he waddled over to a crying Bill. Bill pleaded with the General and soon was bound at the hands and feet. To keep him quiet, Grunt placed a rope in his mouth.

They had increased their night guards to six men now. When the last shift woke the men early the next morning, Bill was alive, but barely. Zebulon came over to him and crouched down with his elbows on his knees with a knife. He cut the rope from his mouth and spoke.

"No woman deserves or should ever go through that. You, on the other hand, deserve what you get. Let's move out. They won't pursue us once they find what they're looking for."

They followed the course of the river in a northwest direction. Bill lay in the dirt, his lower half covered in blood. He squirmed and tried to free himself while yelling to the group, begging for mercy that would not come.

"You god damn sonsofbitches," he yelled. "Untie me, you bastards."

A few hours later, a squadron of Kaw, double their previous number, came across the near-lifeless body. Bound and bloody, he arrived back to their village at night. At the same time, a thousand miles away, his daughter readied herself for bed. She said prayers for the man she would never see or hear from again.

Continuing north, they arrived at a high bluff. The river rushed fifty feet below them, allowing the boy some introspective motivation. The boy's mind was previously flooded with guilt. Now as he stood inanimate, staring at the water, he bordered with not caring at all. The violence of this region was ever present and began to feel somewhat normal.

They often came upon cottonwood trees. High up in the branches lay the bodies of dead Sioux Natives. Adults and children alike were all carefully bundled up in buffalo robes and tied to strong branches with a knife, necklace, or some other personal item sitting against the trunk of the tree. The company saw old lodges that sat black and charred, courtesy of some enemy war party. The embers of the fires were still warm and kept the company on high alert. They passed the ruins of ancient villages that still sat along the river. The sites once were constant reminders of the various cultures and peoples that had inhabited this land. Now they were mere landmarks for men heading west.

They came to a spacious opening where a river called the Platte met with the Missouri. Muddy, turbid waters mixed in with even muddier water. Zebulon stood motionless, with his hands on his hips, at the confluence of these rivers. The company by now had become used to this type of indecisiveness and poor planning by the General. They looked at one another in silent anticipation. Behind them, the loud roaring of the rushing waters raged on.

"We not headed up to the Council Bluffs?" Roger asked, finally breaking the silence.

"Not . . . sureeee," said Zebulon as he twirled his mustache.

By now, he had regained his typical manners, and his smile had returned. He was not a man to dwell on the past. He pulled out his map and flipped it open with a loud snapping noise. He studied it for a moment and spoke again.

"The Platte cuts clear across the plains and right to the Rocky Mountains, while going up the Missouri is a longer journey that takes us near the Arikara, and I would most like to avoid them. Hmm. Aha."

He walked over to a beautiful, dark-orange cottonwood tree and snapped a piece of a branch off it. The company sat back and watched him. Some with annoyance, and others with amused smiles on their faces. He twirled it in his hand as he walked over to the river and crouched down. He submerged one end of the branch in the water, waving it around to ensure it was soaked. He stood and after taking a few steps back from the river, spun the stick in the air. When it first landed, the wet end faced the General. He cursed and performed the ritual again. This time it slightly faced toward the Platte River. He gave a thunderous clap and opened his hands to the sky, as if he had performed some sort of a miracle. He turned toward his less-than-impressed men and spoke to them.

"Does anyone find flaw with going up the Platte route?"

Roger spat. "It's November now, and it'll get mighty snowy, but I reckon we can take up winter with the Pawnee."

"My plan precisely," said Zebulon. "According to this map, they are about one hundred miles up the river. Let's head out!"

The company kept moving and followed the south bank. The river was over a quarter of a mile wide, and the water was murky and dreary like coffee with cream added. In the water were numerous snags and downed trees that made canoe and boat travel all but impossible. The standing trees were mostly bare, having lost their leaves for the approaching winter. Each morning, the ground was covered by a layer of frost that seemed to get thicker each day. The company began to collectively groan of chilliness and hunger. This group of men that represented different races and backgrounds now shared in nothing else but misery. Each time the hunters returned with no sizeable game, this misery compounded.

Naturally, the men became irritable. They began to blame

their misfortunes on various causes. The tracking skills of one man, the body odor of another, or even, most comically, the heavy "footsteps of the half-breeds." They bickered and quarreled like children over the most trivial matters. One evening, the hunters again returned to a dismal fire with empty hands and stomachs. The men all sat around and traded complaints to one another.

"There ain't even a damn rat out here! If we don't get some food, we gone have to make chow outta them horses," said Roger.

"I ain't eatin' a horse," said the boy, and this was echoed by several others.

"You gone eat what you get," Roger replied.

The horses had been picking at dead grass that lacked nutrition. Because of this, their once strong, robust appearances had faded. Thin, delicate bodies now began to show signs of hunger and fatigue. The men continued to grumble until the General stepped in. He sat with legs crossed and had an elegant purple robe draped over him.

"Fret not, men! We shall reach the Pawnee village tomorrow, and I am sure they will be more than thrilled to rescue us from our misery."

As if on cue to shoot down his optimism, small flurries of snow began to become visible as they dove into the fire.

"There ain't no buffalo, no deer, elk, nothin'! And what's worse, the firewood ain't worth a damn, either!" said Roger. He stared at the dried buffalo dung they used for fuel. His frustrations were silently concurred with by all the men except one. Carl lay on his blanket and was wrapped tightly in his robe, using his saddle for a pillow. The soft smile on his face suggested that he was not suffering at all.

"And what the hell you smilin' for?" Roger asked.

"Should I not be smiling?" His breath smelled of whiskey, and he now sat up and stared at Roger. Large snowflakes floated down hard and landed in Roger's beard.

"I don't see a damn thing funny about this here situation. If we get rubbed out, that means you ain't livin' no more, neither."

"Well, if we so happen to die, what would be the use in spending your last few hours complaining and unhappy?"

"It's natural for a man to complain," said Roy as he cut into the conversation. "The problem is when he don't find himself doin' nothin' about it."

Roger ignored Roy's interjection and replied back to Carl.

"I don't think you ever been at want for chow and in the wilderness on crimpy days. Well, this old coon has, and I can tell ye, it ain't a pretty death, to freeze like that. It's only right for a man to holler about it, how else will he know that he wants better?"

"Ain't no use in it, Roger. Not only are we men, we are resourceful, strong. There's no need to worry and gripe."

"So no matter what the situation, you suggestin' we stay positive?"

"I suffered more hardship than you know. Life will chuck negative situations on you, and you'd do best to forget the bad and focus on the good."

The others mocked him and his position.

"And what's so good about this?" said Roger.

"As it stands, we aren't dead yet, and we are here to be able to talk. I never laid eyes on the Rocky Mountains and am excited to see them . . ."

He droned on and on about the beautiful scenery, the prospect of achieving food the next day, and the warmth of the coming sun, until Roger stopped him.

"You just ain't hit yer limit yet. Every man has a limit. I can tell you ain't never suffered through nothin' real."

"Oh, wise one," Carl joked.

"What's your story then?" Roger asked him.

"If you must know, I was born back east in Boston. The first years of my life were ideal. I went to school and joined my father in the insurance business by the time I was only seventeen. After a few years, I became quite good with it, and one time he sent me away to North Carolina on a business trip. Father and I were much alike at the time, hardheaded, tough, stubborn, and we would argue often. We had not spoken for three days when I left and, to be honest, I don't recall what we even argued about."

Here, he paused and laughed before continuing.

"Well, I was gone for about a week when I received message that my poor father had been killed in a gambling hall of all places, by some robbers. I went back up to Boston, and naturally the death of my dear father struck me hard. I never had the chance to talk to him again, to make amends with him. I quit the business and wandered around the states for a few years with nothin' to keep me company but this here bottle."

He unveiled a flask from under his saddle and opened it. He sipped just enough to keep him buzzed and then replaced it where it had been.

"You know what I learned in all my travels? There ain't no point to life. You live, and then you die. And when you die, the world will spin whether your loved ones want it to stop or not. You beg for some God to slow it down so we can have a moment to really grieve our loss, but it doesn't."

He grabbed the bottle again and turned it upward, leaning his head far back. He smiled again after drinking it and continued.

"I could die any day, at any moment, doing anything. A group of savages can ambush us right now, but me sitting up worrying about it won't change anything. You might as well enjoy every moment now while you have the chance. No matter how small, 'cause if I spent the rest of my life angry 'cause something bad happened, I'd regret it on my deathbed. If there ain't no point to this thing, no end goal, you'd do best to enjoy it. You deal with your pain how you choose, and I will with mine."

His hearty laugh scared the boy as Carl again cocooned himself under his robe. He placed that same smile on his face and closed his eyes.

"We'll arrive at the Pawnee and all your fretting will be for nothing," he said before he closed his mouth and spoke no more. Roger scoffed at him but did not retort.

"He told you," Roy joked.

Early the next morning, a torrential blizzard roused the boy before the wake-up call went out. His face was covered with large flakes and frozen stiff. The men attempted the daunting task of traveling in this storm. The wind heaved heavy snowflakes in a horizontal direction. Gusts of wind howled by the company, some strong enough to nearly sweep a man off his mount. The white powder covered their robes and coats. By noon, the starving horses attempted to high step in more than a foot of snow. The remaining bark from the cottonwood trees was not enough to renew the animals. The men looked just as pathetic and found it difficult to sit up straight in their saddles as they rode on.

The warmth of the sun began to abandon the men when they came to where the Loup River joins the Platte. For three miles, they ascended this river without energy or strength to spare among them. When they saw the Pawnee village, they jumped for joy and looked to be a completely different company. Zebulon sent the boy and Old Roy to the village, and they rode side by side and spoke when the wind allowed them to.

"Are the Indins really nicer to us 'cause we're Negroes?" the boy asked.

"Seems to be, but don't think nothin' of it. Some of them Indins back east will act just like the white folk just so they can be accepted. I heard about some of them Cherokee havin' slaves, too."

"Really?"

"All them books you read, and you still don't know nothin,'" Roy joked to the boy.

Soon they arrived at the village, eager for food and warmth. The bright smiles that were exchanged between the two immediately faded away. Their eyes shot wide and dim at what they had seen. When they returned to the company, Roy gave the grim news to the frostbitten men.

"Zebulon," he hesitated.

"Well, out with it, were you well received?" the General asked while shivering.

"There ain't no Pawnee, Cheyenne, Sioux, or 'Rapaho at that village and don't look to have been for about two weeks now."

7

A Harsh Winter

ll around them, nothing moved, neither bird nor mammal. Snow was stacked high around the banks of the Loup River and its islands. All around the destitute group, the country was solid white. Now little more than flurries fell from the sky. In an instant, God's country took the appearance of a wasteland where their graves would sit. The superficial strength and energy they had felt now left the entire group. All but one cursed and expressed their grief. Carl took another sip from his flask and laughed. Roger dismounted his horse, ran wide legged in the knee-high snow, and seized Carl by the robe. He pulled the man down from his horse into the snow and began to assault him. He was able to get off several strong punches before the men could break up the two.

Carl laughed even harder and spit out blood while Roger continued to curse and berate him. Noticeably absent from this struggle was General Zebulon. He turned a bright-red color, began to breathe short, quick breaths, and appeared ready to explode at any moment. Whispers of desertion began to circle the group. Men desired to head back to St. Louis before this man who "couldn't tell a possum from a house cat" would have them all dead.

The General took one long, deep breath. He separated himself, the boy, and Old Roy from the group while the rest of the company grumbled. The General turned his back to the company and spoke. His voice cracked with nervousness as he attempted to whisper.

"I'll put it straight to you two, we are in trouble, as you both know. Without the Pawnee, we will not be able to make it through the winter, which looks to be a strong one. Chances are, they have followed the Platte and are going to their winter quarters. I chose you for your youth and strength, and you, Roy, for your strength, great leg, and wisdom. I need you two to ride ahead at Godspeed and find the Pawnee before we all perish out here. Can I trust the two of you?"

"I don't know," the boy said. "Don't you think Roger would be better?" He looked back at Roger, who glared at Carl as he attempted to catch snowflakes in his bruised mouth.

The General's face grew angry, as did his voice.

"I will not have my expedition end in this manner and be ridiculed by all of St. Louis."

He now caught his anger and softened his speech.

"These men have families that want to see them again, as do you. You have proven yourself as a valuable member of this party. You are young and can ride and run with the best of them, so just listen to everything Roy tells you, and you will be fine. Whatever it takes, find them. We will head back down to the Platte and wait for you."

The boy looked uneasy, but he and Roy immediately set back down the Loup River and traveled west when they came back to the Platte. Wrapped tightly in his robe, the boy's body was quite warm. His feet were still exposed to the cold and began to enter the first phase of frostbite. He would shake his toes occasionally and noticed how it became more difficult each time. The sun began to retreat to the west now, and his teeth began a violent chatter at the loss of its warmth.

"Just don't think about it," Roy would say. This annoyed the boy to no end, as he didn't know how to not think about it. A bitter, bone-chilling cold that was impossible to ignore swept over them.

Roy sat tall on his horse. It almost seemed as if the glacial temperatures were not bothering him. The boy often cut his eye at Roy and thought he could not be human to withstand such freezing temperatures and the gusting wind that accompanied them. Roy was statuesque, and not once did he comment on any discomfort, and this gave the boy an extra push to continue.

Two days of travel passed with still no signs of the Pawnee. Extreme hunger began to cripple the boy. His head began to spin, and he was forced to grab ahold of the saddle's pommel just to remain sitting up straight. He caught a glimpse of Roy having to do the same thing. The man finally showed a chink in his armor, and this made the boy relax a little. If he was weak, then he wasn't weak alone.

That night, they sat in an area they had cleared with a small fire fueled by buffalo dung in front of them. The journey was miserable during the day, but the small warmth of the sun helped the boy feel that he could go on. But when night closed in on them, the freezing temperatures were unbearable. On this night especially, the boy felt his very soul begin to rattle. He sat cross-legged with the robe curtained over him. Months earlier, he had complained about the stifling heat and humidity of New Orleans. Now, he wished for nothing more than to feel it again.

The thought alone provided him with a temporary moment of relief. When the wind gusted pass him, it took the relief with it. Roy sat much in the same manner and spoke to him.

"I never did get where you were from."

It took the boy a few seconds to answer. He didn't want to talk but realized that maybe it would take his mind off the cold.

"Te- . . . Tennessee."

"Oh? Likewise. What's your story? How do you come to be out here in the freezing cold?"

The boy hesitated for a moment. He thought about the murders and wondered if the law would still be looking for him. No matter how much he trusted Roy, it was best to keep his secret a secret.

"I got into an argument with my parents."

"So you run away to the wilderness? What was that about?"

"Well, they don't wanna let me live my own life. They keep saying I'm gonna follow in my paw's footsteps, and I don't want to live like him."

"Your paw is a free man?"

"Yes. He bought his freedom and my ma's. I got three siblings, and we was all born free, too. Paw bought some land in Tennessee and made a lot of money when the white folks bought some of it off him."

"A wealthy, free black man with a loving family that wants nothing but the top for his boy. What's wrong with that again?"

"It ain't for me. I can't be happy like that."

"Well, pup, I hate to stick my finger in your coffee, but we may die out here, anyway, so I'll say it. You don't know a blessing when it looks you in the face."

"They the reason I ended up out here. If it weren't for them, I wouldn't have . . ."

Here the boy interrupted himself but had he not, Roy certainly would have.

"They ain't the reason for that. I don't care how old you are, you ain't nobody's child no more. You see, that's the measure of a man, to see what is responsible for his own life and do somethin' about it. You made the choice to come out here, and if you die out here, the fault is yours not theirs. Blamin' your parents for the choices you made only shows weakness and that you ain't a man yet. And if you don't understand that, I can see why your parents still wanna guide you along your path."

"But what's the measure of a man when you can't even go out in public without showing some white man your pass? . . . Roy, I just wanna travel, see the world, but they don't understand that and pushed me away."

"Your paw was a slave, and if he lived anything like me, he's seen many families separated, little ones cryin' out for they mama, and they would never see her again. He sees the way he made somethin' of himself against the odds, so when his boy come to him sayin' how he don't want to be like him, it hurts a man. You ever thought from his eyes?"

"No." The boy lowered his head in shame.

"Maybe you should, you'll see he only wants the best for you. Big landowner in Tennessee, you say? What's your pappy's name?"

"James."

"Big dark man? With a scar on his forehead?"

"How do you know him?"

"Ain't too many free blacks that will do what your papa do. He is more of a man than you know. Back when I was still in slavery . . . I was never nobody's slave, so I was 'in slavery.' I began to do a little carpentry work to try to buy my freedom. It was gonna take me a mighty long time, so I heard about a man who would help the slaves buy they freedom. You put up half, and he give you the other half with no strings. If he didn't help, many others wouldn't be free today."

The boy sat stunned for a moment. He and his father were close, best friends even, but he had never heard of this. He felt embarrassed that this man held his father in higher esteem than he seemed to. Roy continued.

"My sister, Queen, lived on the same plantation. She was all I had left after everybody else died or got sold off. I wanted to buy her freedom, but you see, she caught a sickness and told me not to waste my money since she was gonna go under, anyway. When she did die, I instantly felt regret for not allowin' her to taste freedom at least for one day. She was all I had in the world, and I sometimes still feel like I failed her."

Roy stared into the dim fire before he continued.

"Got off topic, but you know what my biggest regret is? I never had a family of my own. Why do you think I'm an old man out here? You think I like bein' cold and starving? No, this here is a young man's life. Of course, I love the adventure of it, but I'd much rather be sittin' with some little chilluns runnin' round. I'm sure your paw is the same. A man don't measure up to much without his family. Don't forget that."

Before the boy could register a response, a sound of crunching snow came close behind him. His heart thumped in his chest and terror alleviated his body of the numbness he had been feeling. Large gray wolves scavenged and terrorized the area. The boy was sure a pack of them now came to collect their much-needed meal. The low sound continued to inch closer until Roy saw what caused it. He slowly grabbed his rifle and gave the boy a command not to move as he trained it over the boy's right shoulder. Roy spoke in a low whisper.

"Lean your head to your left," he said.

The deafening boom of the gun echoed throughout the river valley, and the boy's body dropped to the ground. He threw his hands to his neck, felt for blood, and was relieved to find none. He sat up and looked at a mass of dark fur belonging to a young buffalo that lay dead behind him. Its eyes were still open, and it stared into the fire, and the two exclaimed and jumped up in exhilaration.

"It must've been separated from its herd and tried to get warm from our fire," Roy said.

They skinned and dressed the calf, and within two hours, their stomachs were full and their spirits renewed. The boy found the cold much more tolerable with the hunger pains gone. Even though the wind continued to howl over them, they still managed to get a few traces of sleep.

The sun brought another chilly morning. The Pawnee had to be close, and today was the day they would find them. The boy rose from his makeshift bed and stretched his tight legs for a moment. His eyes were bright balls of fire as he was eager to start the day's journey. His fire, however, was extinguished when he looked in horror at both of the horses. They lay on their sides with eyes wide open, their bodies stiff, wooden boards. Thoughts of death by starvation and frostbite blew through his mind. A cold, paralyzing gust of wind ripped through the river valley. He panicked and woke Roy.

"They're dead," he cried.

"I'm surprised they made it this long. Looks like we gotta get to movin,'" said Roy, with a yawn as he rose up.

The boy began to sob.

"Nothin' is going right," he said. He scrunched his face.

"Eh, cut that shit. Won't do you a bit of good," Roy barked. His demeanor cradled the boy's fears and caused him to relax.

Ten minutes later, they began their rough trek through the deep snow. By two o'clock that afternoon, another storm of dark, fluffy gray clouds rolled toward them. The wind and snow ravaged them. It was impossible to tell whether they headed to the Pawnee or someplace else. Even the river was shrouded in the whiteout.

Without the meat they ate the previous night and the small pieces they saved for this day, the two would not have been able to continue. The boy's youth and strength did indeed allow him to prevail. For now he felt strong, as the large snowflakes that blew in his face became a mere annoyance. He turned his head behind him to gain relief from the wind and cried out when he saw Roy's body on the ground. He was about fifty feet away and snow was already beginning to pile on him. When the boy reached Roy, he was out of breath after hopping in the knee-deep snow. Frantic, he tossed snow away from Roy, giving him room to breathe.

"Roy, Roy," he yelled. "Get up, we're almost there."

Roy's eyes opened and rolled over the unpigmented landscape.

"Where are we?"

"Hell if I know. We're close to the Pawnee, get up."

"What happened?"

"We are gonna go find the Pawnee and save the company. You the strongest of all of us, and without you, we won't make it."

Such a compliment gave Roy what he needed to rise to his feet, and with the boy's help, he was able to do just that. Roy was shorter than the boy but not noticeably. In his old age, he had begun to shrink a little. The boy set Roy's arm over his back and supported the man's aged and sturdy body. The two crawled at a snail's pace and had not gone twenty feet before Roy's legs gave out on him, and he collapsed again. They continued in this way for the rest of the day, and that night the boy did not see sleep at all. He instead sat perched over Roy, kept heavy, concerned eyes over him, and woke him at intervals.

The next morning, the two repeated the same process. They finished off what was left of the calf's lean meat the night before. Hunger, along with supporting Roy, began to affect the boy. By now his legs were wet noodles. His entire body screamed at him to stop whatever was causing the discomfort.

For a while, he led an intense battle in his mind against negative and defeated thoughts. He formed a thick wall and kept those thoughts outside of it, but this protective barrier would not last. Eventually the defeating thoughts found a crack in his barrier. This was the beginning of the end, as he and Roy both collapsed together and would not rise. The boy's voice shook and scratched, and he stared at Roy who looked to be upside down.

"Roy?"

"Yeah?"

"I wanna go home."

"Me too, pup, me too."

Peace. Peace is what the boy felt when he closed his eyes. He always thought that dying would be accompanied by screaming and crying, but he stared at the inside of his eyelids and for the first time in months, his soul was still. Minutes later, he opened his eyes again and stared up at the gray sky as those thick clouds floated by. He lifted his head slightly and looked to his left. Roy was being carried on a wooden cot by two men that were heavily wrapped in animal fur. Then he shut his eyes again and felt nothing but the bumps that came along with the men's footsteps.

When he opened his eyes again, he expected to see a faceless God sitting high on some throne, judging him. Instead he saw a large fire that burned at the center of a spacious tipi. He looked over and saw Roy. He was missing his bandanna. His woolly gray hair spiraled in random directions.

A man entered the tipi and removed his robe, allowing his dark hair to flow down to his shoulders. He sung to himself in his language, carried a clay bowl in his hand, and walked over to the two. He set the bowl down in front of the boy. He studied them both, and when he saw that Roy was still out, he pulled what looked to be a large cigarette from his belt. He lit the end of it over the fire and waved it under Roy's wide nostrils for a few seconds. Roy jumped awake and, with curious eyes, looked to be new to the world.

The man picked up the red-and-yellow clay bowl, took a spoonful of cornmeal from it, and fed it to them both. After they chewed and swallowed, he grabbed them both and made them stand up. He led them in some aerobic exercise until sweat began to glisten off their skin. When fatigue started to set in, the man sat them down. He fed them another spoonful and then made them rise again. They continued this for a few more rotations until their strength returned. When a bowl of dried deer jerky was brought to them, they tore away at it like a pack of rabid wolves.

The man then crouched down and stared directly into the face of the boy. The two were remarkably similar in complexion. The biggest difference between them was the man's shoulder-length hair that told of his Cherokee heritage. To add even more confusion, he spoke to the two in nearly perfect English.

"You're lucky we found you, for if we hadn't, your bodies would have been recovered in the spring or, worse, ripped apart by the wolves."

Both Roy and the boy thanked him.

"Where are we?" said Roy.

"On the Platte River, among the Pawnee. We were moving to their wintering grounds and stopped here to camp."

The boy's eyes opened wide and he began to panic when he remembered just why he and Roy were out there.

"Our group," he yelled. "We were scouting in advance of a group of trappers. We came to your village but saw that you all left. We gotta go back and get them."

"How many men?" the man asked.

"Twenty-five, thirty."

"Americans?"

"And a few Frenchman, some half-breeds," said Roy.

"I'll talk to the chief."

The Pawnee sent a rescue party out toward the east. Each man had firewood strapped on his back. They carried dried fish, buffalo meat, and berries. They braved the treacherous conditions and found the party in a pitiful condition. They had continued west and not made more than five miles' progress. Eight of their animals were frozen stiff and carefully preserved in ice. Many others were carved and hacked to pieces, their flesh having been scavenged by the starving company.

The General refused to eat a horse, claiming it was "beneath him." He in particular sat in a starved and terrible condition. His face was gaunt, and his spirit all but frozen over. If the company had not been found, he might not have lasted another two days. A week later, the company hobbled into the Pawnee encampment and received warm welcomes with shouts of joy. Five days after their arrival, the company had regained its strength. They continued westward with the Pawnee toward their wintering grounds.

They arrived two days later and found the white landscape dotted with tipis and small fires. The children were balls of fur in their winter clothing. They ran around playing with dogs in this peaceful setting.

By now, Zebulon had regained his robustness and eccentricity. He styled his hair in typical fashion, and his peculiar manner of speech returned to him. At the camp, he was introduced to a large chief whose name was given in English as "White Hair." The tall man looked the General in the eye, shook his cautious hand, and gave his welcome to the company.

The short dark man who had nursed the boy and Roy back to health stood between the General and White Hair. He looked up at the both of them and translated their messages to each other.

His name was Charles, and he was of mixed ancestry. His father was Scottish while his mother was mixed with Cherokee and Negro. He grew up in American society but had spent the better part of the last ten years among various Native tribes. The man was an invaluable resource. He knew several languages as well as the customs of the Natives and whites, intimately.

Despite being treated well, Zebulon stood blatantly uncomfortable in White Hair's presence. The Pawnee seemed to never take issue with this. White Hair invited the company to spend the entire winter there with them. The General had no choice but to accept, and they spent the next couple of months in procuring more horses, beans, pumpkins, corn, cured meat, and most of all, beaver pelts.

On one of these excursions, the boy learned the process from Henry. They ascended a small stream not far from the forks of the river. Henry grabbed a previously killed beaver and lifted its tail, under which hung a small sac. He stripped a small piece of bark off of a tree and doused it with some of the oil from the sac. Next, he attached the bark to a metal trap. He placed the assembly near a five-foot-high beaver dam.

"They are a territorial animal, no doubt about that," Henry said. "One will smell that and wonder who is sniffing around its area and will check it out, then bam." He made a thunderous clap with his hands and startled the boy. "We got ourselves a beaver."

They placed six traps in this fashion going up the stream. They returned later that day, and five large carcasses were drowned in the water. Nothing was seen at the sixth trap, but as the boy walked closer, he could see that it had been set off. The boy leisurely lowered his feet into the freezing water. He picked up the trap, which held only the left leg of a beaver in its jaws.

"Ho, Henry," the boy said as he brought the trap over to him. "I think this one sprung too hard and chopped his leg off."

Henry grabbed the trap and examined the leg with great curiosity. He smiled as he began to speak.

"No. Sometimes you come across a creature that wants to be free more than you want to catch it. They'll go to amazing measures to retain that freedom, and the fat rat bit its own leg off to have that. He's hopping around here somewhere."

"It chewed off its own leg? I don't know if I could do that."

"I hope to think that you would. That beaver has known what it is to be free, so when someone tried to steal that from it, it's no surprise what he'd go through to keep it. That's why we have respect for them animals, they ain't much more different than us."

The boy stared at the leg. He pictured the law coming for his freedom and him having to cut off his ankle to remain free. He shuttered at the thought.

"You were born . . . eh, um, a slave, right?" he asked Henry.

"My body was, yes, but my spirit always knew that I was more."

"How'd you make it out here, then?"

Henry smiled and revealed a great set of white teeth. When he spoke, his mighty voice carried all up and down the stream.

"I was born in the woods of Georgia, in a sweaty, miserable excuse for a home. I think I was around ten years old when my so-called master, who had to have been crafted by Lucifer himself, a man named Thomas Mills, took me to St. Louis. Now this was just when the government purchased it, so I'd say around the year of our Lord eighteen hundred and five, maybe? Well, naturally I hated every minute of that lifestyle, but I knew nothing else so I stuck with it, but my soul always ached. By chance, one of the house gals overheard a conversation between Thomas and his wife.

"He was getting older and, like all of them, began to feel bad about his exploits only after he reaped a life of benefits from them. In his will, it was written for myself and many more of us to be free upon his death. Now I was no killer, but I believe the Lord put a plan in my heart that day. I used to drive a wagon, and you see I spent a lot of time with Thomas, so on one of our trips, I poisoned his water. Now I'm a churchgoing man, always have been and always will be, but boy, did I smile as he drank it. He didn't fall ill until we returned back to the plantation, which was just as well due to suspicion, but two days later, he died a slow, painful death. I played a sad role better than anyone and a week after that, his wife called us all together and told us that she was going back to her family in Georgia and that we were free. I haven't looked back since."

Something inside the boy was roused by the story and a wide smile sat on his face. A piece of history stood in front of him. Henry would be persecuted now but celebrated hundreds of years later. Henry had stood up to the insurmountable wall that was slavery. Like that beaver, he did what he had to do to remain free.

"Were you nervous?"

"Not in the least, because I know that a Negro that plays the fool can get away with murder," he laughed.

"But do you regret having to kill someone?"

The question was selfish in nature, as the boy now turned somber and thought about his own soul. He hoped that a certain answer from Henry would alleviate him of any guilt.

"I do wish that I never had to. It takes a special kind of madness to wake up and want to kill a man but like that beaver, look at the situation I was in. God gave every man the right to freedom and to live his life in peace, and any man try to take that from you? I like to think that He would understand your actions. Now, let's get back to camp, it's getting dark."

The boy stood motionless with the trap and the beaver's leg in his hands. He respected the animal and admired its courage and fearlessness. The beaver was indeed just like the boy, longing for the same feelings of freedom and security. He rationalized that leaving home was him chewing off his own leg in an attempt to achieve freedom. Henry had done the same when he poisoned his slave master. Due to this, the boy gave the beaver the name of Henry and hoped to see him again.

All winter long, the company's camp intertwined with the Pawnee's. The two groups mingled, hunted, ate, and leisured together. The Pawnee were overly generous in their attempts to make friends out of the "pale faces." The company was just as generous in their efforts to survive a harsh winter in a region inhabited by a population that could understandably act cruel toward them.

Day after day, parties of Pawnee returned to the camp with dozens of dog-sized beaver carcasses. For their efforts, they were given large volumes of whiskey. The boy caught sight of Roger coating the bottom of a measuring cup with melted buffalo fat. This cheap trick gave the appearance of more whiskey in the cup than was present.

The General gave orders to not become too preoccupied with the drink and to "stay ever on guard when a savage is near." Of course, the men paid no attention to this rule. At night, the company and the Pawnee alike would transform a quiet wintering ground into a circus. One night in particular provided the following scenery:

Blood was everywhere and stained the once-untouched snow-banks. Men from the company and the Pawnee all clashed in fights around the encampment. James and the boy were bent over at the waist, attempting to wrestle each other to the ground. Bloodied and bruised, the two growled at each other like wolves. They collided and James's legs gave way. The boy scooped him up and drove him to the ground, eliciting loud, drunken cheers from onlookers. Roger tossed a Pawnee man into a tipi, gazed up at the sky, and howled at the glowing moon. The aroma and sound of gunshots lingered around the camps. Distraught mothers covered the ears of their screaming children well into the night. At the night's conclusion, bodies lay everywhere. Some were found near their tents, others on the banks of the river half frozen. All the while, the General sat in his tent. He tightly clutched his pistol and stared at the tent flap, awaiting whatever was to enter.

The company lived as the Natives would and slept under the hide of the tipis. They wore and traded for beautifully made moccasins and buckskin shirts. Many of the whites grew their hair long and from afar, they looked to be Natives themselves. They even began to pick up small traces of the Pawnee language. When they spoke it, the Pawnee would laugh softly at the pronunciations.

The Pawnee picked up words and phrases such as ball, lead, powder, rifle, and son of a bitch. They beamed with pride at their mastery over what they deemed were the most-important words to white men. Every aspect of the Pawnee lifestyle was readily allocated to the company save one. The Pawnee women were exotic to the company, many of whom had never ventured this far west. The men attempted to court some of them in the name of strengthening the "red-white alliance."

James Calloway had begun to boast to the boy about a young Pawnee woman to whom he had taken a liking. She was no older than eighteen, sturdy, and her beauty coerced James to begin to sneak into her tent on nights when her husband was not there. He did not speak her language, nor her his, but his nonverbal intentions were without question and she appeared to feel the same. One night after one of his trips to her lodge, James sat in a tipi with the boy and Jacques. They drank whiskey and engaged in general chatter when the General burst in. His eyes were set on James almost as if the boy and Jacques were not in the room. The General plopped down in front of James and crossed his legs.

"General Zebulon, what can I do ya fer?" asked James.

"James, if I were to perish today, would a man in, let's say Brazil, know the name of Argan Zebulon and mourn?"

"What's that?"

"The question was simple. If I were to die today, would a man in Brazil mourn for me?"

James looked at the boy who exchanged a puzzled expression with Jacques.

"I guess not?"

"Exactly. Now, I am a simple man and want but two things in my life, those being fame and abundant riches. I am on the cusp of both and don't intend on having my fabulous story told by others rather than myself."

"What're you talking about, General?" asked James.

The boy watched in silence.

"That little savage you have been sneaking off to see and spending time with? I am almost certain you know her to be White Hair's newest wife."

"He won't find out a thing. She and I . . ."

"These are a treacherous and dangerous people without giving them reason to be. So imagine if he were to find out about your transgressions. We would all lose our hair and, yes, even you," he said pointing to the boy. "I will kill you myself before I allow you to jeopardize my life's work. Do you understand?"

"Yes, sir."

The General stood, made James rise up, and hugged him as if he had just finished scolding his son. He then nodded his head to the boy and Jacques and, just like that, he was gone without saying another word.

Christmas, the New Year, and several more weeks passed and

it was now early February. Beavers were being brought back in such large quantities that the company found it difficult to leave the region. They decided to meet with the Pawnee before doing so.

When the boy, the General, Charles, Roy, and Roger all entered an extremely large tipi, they were met by three Pawnee men. Each was ornamented with brilliant jewelry and draped in fine, colorful deerskin robes. Each of the three sat regal with legs crossed. They wore their hair long and slicked to the back, revealing their high cheekbones and large faces. An air of elegance and dignity surrounded the men, and the boy thought that if people from back east could see this, they would not call them savages. Or maybe they still would? The General and the rest of the company saw the Natives the same as the boy did. Yet they still used the word savage almost every five minutes.

Sitting at the center of the trio was the chief, whose authority reigned supreme. Deep-set wrinkles on his face offered a hint of his elder status over the other two, as well as his wisdom. He looked to be frail and gentle, but when he spoke, his great voice still commanded attention. His voice was one that would cause any man to want to sit down and hear what he had to say. It had a calming effect, as did the tranquility of the meeting, which soothed the boy. He looked over at the General. The outline of his clenched jaw protruded from his face. Charles spoke to only the middle chief, whose English name was given as Moon Chief. He was a man who frequently boasted on being accustomed to the ways of the "pale faces."

"He says that you are one of the good ones," said Charles.

Zebulon hesitated for a moment before replying.

"He is one of the great ones."

Moon Chief smiled.

"They say that although spring is coming soon, it isn't wise to head to the mountains now," said Charles.

"Is it possible?"

"Yes. But why risk it? The two parties have enjoyed a prosperous winter here together and many more beaver are to be trapped."

"So other men have done so, even earlier in the year?" said General Zebulon.

"Yes, and others have not."

"All the more reason to go." Zebulon sat up straight and a look of fire shot through his eyes. "Other men have done more with less, and if spring will be here soon, the worst is behind us."

Charles relayed the message, and Moon Chief's face colored with disappointment.

"He says a single storm can cause you and your entire party to perish."

"That won't be so. I've made up my mind to this. Now I only ask for the best route to take."

Moon Chief was quiet and gathered the two other chiefs, who leaned together and spoke in their tongue.

"What? What are they saying?" said Zebulon. His face became even tenser, and he raised an eyebrow.

"You must relax, General," said Charles with a smile. "They say you won't find much in the way of fuel until you reach the forks of the Platte. When you find yourself here, take the southern route. It has more firewood."

General Zebulon sprang to his feet and bent at the waist to each of the three chiefs. He thanked them, donned his robe, and exited the tipi in a hurry. The chiefs were clearly amused by the General's antics, and White Hair spoke for the first time.

The two others laughed at his joke as the company sat in an awkward silence.

"What'd he say?" the boy asked Charles.

"Ah, it's not important."

The next morning brought a sun so bright that the boy could not keep his eyes open. It was accompanied by a much-needed heat that warmed the boy enough that he removed his robe. The cold breeze on his hot head soothed him. He sat upon one of the fifty-five new horses that the General had purchased and traded for. He ran his hands along its short, cotton-soft gray coat and sat up high on the tall stallion. He looked up at hordes of Pawnee that came to see off the men. Some with sadness, and others with glee. A young woman brought the boy new pairs of moccasins. She gave a shy smile when he took them and thanked her. After berating him for his newfound love interest, the company was ready to head farther west.

The General, covered in a vest made of buffalo fur, sat catlike in his saddle, looking noble and important. He turned up his nose to everything and everyone around him. He spoke quiet positive affirmations to and about himself as he made the call to ride out. Charles had been convinced to join the company as an interpreter. He spoke to an elder Pawnee man. The man pointed toward the mountains, then to the sun, and then to the river, which had already begun to rise. Charles shrugged his shoulders and cupped the man's hands in his and bid the man farewell. He brought his horse up to a trot and took his place alongside the General.

8

The General's Secret

he day of the departure could not have been any more ideal. Spring appeared to be near, and the company was in high spirits and hoped to reach the mountains in two weeks. Melted snow dripped as water from the branches of the trees. The entire countryside appeared to be in one big thaw. The grass would rise from under its winter blanket, as would the temperatures. Each day would become easier than the previous. They would make their way to the mountains and all perform a celebratory dance at the quantities of beaver they found there. But such a fate would only follow a leader who was humble enough to take heed to warnings. Argan Zebulon was not such a leader.

The next day, temperatures plummeted as thick, wintry clouds rolled in and covered the sun. Bitter prairie winds swept over and delivered painful stings to exposed skin. The cold gusts stopped the horses dead in their tracks. Had Charles not convinced the General to carry firewood, the entire company would have frozen over. Each morning a horse was found either too cold to stand or deceased, and the riders were not much better off. Each groaned and complained about their situation except Carl. He and the General began to bond over their optimistic outlooks. Not even the snow, which was over two and a half feet high, could dampen the spirits of these two men. The company's progress was a crawl in comparison to their normal advancement. They continued in this way for over two weeks until they at last came to the forks of the Platte River.

They elected to ascend the south fork of the river. Yet again, they were pummeled with another violent storm of blustering winds and snow that fell in what seemed to be five-inch increments.

About a mile down the South Platte River, they came upon a portion of the valley that was covered by an uncountable amount of buffalo. In search for food, they not only trampled a path but also revealed the grass underneath. At night, many of the beasts would cozy as close to the company's fire as possible and made easy hunting for the men.

Though they had grass, the weary horses began to drag their feet. The boy began to switch the packs between his two horses more frequently. When they came to an island with a grove of cottonwood trees, the men dropped to the ground in praise of the Almighty. The weather began to relent its cruel treatment of the company, and there they made camp. On a clear, beautiful day, they looked to the west and saw the jagged and snowcapped peaks of the Rocky Mountains. The boy bowed down to their grandeur and beauty, and in this, he was not alone.

There they camped for five days, while their horses scoured the bark of the trees and in time regained their stamina and youthful appearances. They continued down the South Platte without incident and came to a section of hills that stood at the base of the mountains.

The boy stood in awe at their towering appearance. For the first time in a while, he thought about his mother. She wouldn't believe how amazing this view was. He had never felt so small, and in this moment, he realized his insignificance in the greater scheme of the world. For a moment, he grew sad. He had now been gone from home for over five months. He had seen more in these months than most had seen in a lifetime. But the people he wanted to tell about his adventures were almost a thousand miles from him. They had no clue as to his whereabouts or even if he was alive.

He longed for conversations with his father and to hear his mother's laughter. To take his mind off this, he ascended some of the hills with the General. The two overlooked an astounding country to the east. Melting snow and ice glazed the hillside, and the sound of water that dripped from the pine needles made incessant pats against the snow-covered ground it fell on. Herds of slow-moving buffalo trudged along the bottom of the hills, while antelope galloped along the prairie. To the west behind them, snow-capped and ominous loomed the high peaks of the mountains.

The General had his hands on his hips and his head up to the sky. He blew out hot air and watched his breath spiral away from him, and all looked to be right in his world. He walked over to the boy, placed his arm around him, and spoke.

"See? God's country."

"I been wondering. What do the Indins call themselves? Or the land and places?"

An amused look shot across the General's face.

"Does it matter?" he smiled.

The boy said nothing, and they both continued to admire the wide-open terrain.

The company spent a few days trapping streams that fed the river and also in deliberation. They brought in more beaver than they knew what to do with and deliberated their next choice of action. Charles pulled out a map and spoke to the General.

"If you plan on collecting more furs, you're gonna need to send some downriver back to St. Louis or bury some," said Charles.

"Bury some?!," said the General. "Why in God's name would we bury some?"

"Trappers do it all the time, they call it a cache. You find a spot that you think is safe and bury your furs and come back for them later."

The General gave the impression of not trusting Charles's Native blood. He looked over at Roger, who nodded his head in agreement.

"Is there a spot safe in this land? How do I know they won't be plundered?"

"You don't. You either do this or send some men back downriver in a boat to take them back to St. Louis."

The General gave a concerned look.

"Fair enough. But if anything shall happen to these furs, I'll hold you accountable."

"They'll hold up safe. The bigger issue, then, is how to proceed."

"How do you mean? We shall go right over the Rockies."

"That's not a wise idea, General. That high up sees blackbird storms well into spring and snow stays on the caps sometimes into the summer."

"We've made it thus far and only lost horses and mules. I think we men, with our faculties and innovation, can conquer anything that mountain will throw at us."

"I don't think you understand. There is snow packed taller than any man in your party, with temperatures that drop dangerously low. Very few men have ever taken a direct route through the mountains and lived to tell about it."

Charles didn't know that to speak of the dangers was to rouse the General even more. His eyes grew wide when he heard about these potentially perilous situations. He had already overcome several storms on the Platte and seemed eager to add to the adventure story that was his life. However, Charles was quick-witted. He devised another route to change the General's ambitions.

"Well, I know of another route even less taken, with many unnamed landmarks. Hot springs everywhere, rock towers that stand over one hundred men high. I'd rather take you along this route."

The General's eyes lit up even more now, as the boy laughed at the obvious ploy. The men joined together in jeers of "Argan's Tower" and "Zebulon's Hole," among others. Soon they jetted north with the mountains soaring overhead on their left side.

Since the company left the Pawnee camp, they had been on continuous alert for parties of raiding Natives. At night, every gust of wind that creaked a branch and every howl of a wolf were met with a suspicion and a rifle trained in its direction. For a while, they were fortunate enough to not encounter any tangible threat, but this was to be short-lived.

They arrived at the North Platte River, camped on its banks, and began crafting buffalo-hide canoes to cross the river that was usually fordable. The country was overrun with wild sage that they used for their fires. The mountains to the southwest were barely visible now, and looping hills and high bluffs were everywhere around them. Though the sun was now out, the country still held on to the remnants of that harsh winter.

One evening, the company had been hard at work at the task as foretold. Carl, Sammy, and Bradan, who all had become close, returned to the camp with their horses at full gallop. Sammy was especially red in the face, and the trio nearly fell over, out of breath as they attempted to speak at once.

"In- . . . Indins! Coming!"

"Fort up," the General screamed, and the company grabbed their weapons and prepared for a fight.

"How many?" the General asked.

"Two, three hundred at the least!"

Zebulon cursed and he, too, grabbed his rifle and ammunition. With the high river at his back, the boy took up the familiar defensive position. He crouched on one knee and nervously held his gun. Sammy had been quivering so badly that the others from the party kept at least five feet from him. No one wanted to become his next victim of friendly fire. Few trees dotted that open landscape. From miles away, the party of Natives appeared. Already the boy could see that the Natives indeed outnumbered the company by at least ten to one. He took a long gulp as he tried to come to grips that this may be his final day on the earth.

Many of the party's entire faces were painted red with white handprints over their mouths. Handprints were stamped on their naked chests, and many more were distributed over the strong bodies of their menacing horses. Several were dressed in long, bullet-riddled navy blue coats that were trimmed with gold and silver lace. One warrior, so small and young that his buffalo robe covered his entire body. He appeared to be a mound of fur riding on horseback. Another adorned a large headdress with long feathers that looked to come from some ancient beast.

One of the men rode with a hat made from the top of a buffalo's head, with two long horns curving out from either side. They were armed with long sabers that had tasted the flesh of men in countries far and wide. Slung on their backs were rifles that were old, prior to the war. Beautifully crafted bows made of buffalo tusks that were painted light blue and red. Arrows that would whistle through the air as they zoomed toward their targets. And one with a five-pound steel ball that was tethered to a chain. He swung this around the right side of his horse, looking much like the rest of his fellow warriors: dangerous, ferocious, cruel. The boy took another large, nervous gulp as the war party drew closer. Right before he pulled his trigger, they stopped. Five American flags were raised high above the riders and flapped in the wind.

The company gave a collective sigh of relief. James taunted the riders under his breath after they had shown their friendliness. The General gave Grunt a flag to hoist up high as well, and the Natives made their way closer to the camp. They were of the Sioux faction, and their leader, a man called Clawing Bear, spoke to Charles. His eyes would remain fixed on the General throughout the entire conversation.

They spoke of all the typical things men spoke on when they encountered others in the wilderness. Who they were, where they were from, the hardships ahead. While they spoke, many of the Sioux warriors began to dismount their wild-looking horses. They began to walk toward the company's camp. Roger pulled his gun and aimed it at one of the warriors and dared him to move farther. The man did not speak English, but such a gesture and the venom in the words behind it needed no translation. Instantly, a sea of guns and arrows all aimed on the outmanned company. Charles pleaded with Clawing Bear, who gave the order to drop their weapons, as Zebulon's company did the same. The General again was red in the face as he spoke to Charles.

"What the hell was that? What do they want?"

"They say that to promote peaceful relations between the nations, they require gifts."

As he said this, more of the Sioux dismounted and began making their way through the company's camp. The General gritted his teeth and was as red as some of the painted faces of the warriors.

"No need to tell you what will happen if we interfere," said Charles. "This is their land, let them take what they need."

"They have no claim, no deed to any land," the General said. He barked his words, but they had no effect in a land where he was no authority.

They went through tents and rummaged through all they could find. They pulled out personal packs, going through letters, heirlooms, and gifts. They turned over bedding and robes, pots and pans, and anything that looked to be of the slightest use. They carefully examined the horses and mules and spoke among themselves over the muscle structure, age, and use of the animals. Some emerged from the tents with knives, gunpowder, and personal sacks. One of them kneeled at the boy's and pulled out his small metal tin. He extracted the papers inside, holding them up with great curiosity in his large hands.

The thought of his freedom being taken from him overcame the boy. Without thinking, he walked over to him and snatched the tin from him and placed it in his trouser pocket. The man's broad chest was stuck out. He stood tall and imposing while he stared down at the boy, who remained unflinching. Their eyes locked together, and each looked for any slight sign of weakness from the other. When none was found, the man smiled and went about his business and continued to raid elsewhere. When they had finished pillaging, the Sioux walked back to their horses. They carried their tolls as Clawing Bear spoke to Charles.

"He's saying that the Arapaho are near the Black Hills, and they mean harm to any whites attempting to pass."

The General remained quiet as his body shook as he stared at, rather through, Clawing Bear. His gaze showed that his mind was somewhere else. Somewhere far, far away. Clawing Bear toiled to release the words "thank you" to the company as he gave a hubristic smile. Clawing Bear turned his horse to leave. The company watched this perilous group of warriors disappear over the same hills they had come from.

When they were gone, the General became irate. He cursed not only the Sioux but all "Indins" in general. Snow flew ten feet courtesy of his boots as he stomped and kicked everything he could see. He pulled out his pistol and aimed it toward the direction of the departed Sioux. He simulated firing the weapon at them. Grunt came over to the General. With a large claw, he grabbed his arm and the gun from his hand. The General was not the only one to curse the "Indins." These gripes and complaints lasted well into the night, when they sat at a fire and hurled insults at the Sioux and Clawing Bear.

"Them red niggers think they own the land! Who do they think they are to make us pay a price to pass through?" said Roger.

"Savage bastards," said the General. A piece of him had calmed down now, but he was still nearly foaming at the mouth. "Backward and without morals. We bring enterprise and civilization. Medicine, where they chew the roots of trees.

Science, where they have only their primitive beliefs. God, where they have none!"

The half-blooded men in the party were quiet, spoke among themselves, and didn't seem to pay the two any mind.

The boy looked at the General. From the moment he thought of speaking, his heart banged against the inside of his chest, urging him to keep his mouth shut. Through his flamboyance, the General was an intimidating figure after all. Tall, strong, with a dark side to him that seemed to be unraveling the longer they spent time in the wilderness. All this made the boy afraid. But afraid of what? He had been in a battle against Natives and even killed two men who had been intent on wronging him. He had lived through the roughest part of winter out here, and now he sat in fear of this man's opinion? The thought made him chuckle in embarrassment. If he were not ready to even voice his opinion, then was he really worthy of being the man he told his father that he was? If he could not speak up now, then him leaving home and all the heart-wrenching pain and suffering that came from it would have been for nothing.

"You speak as if whites have done no wrong in this country," the boy said with a shaky voice. When the sky did not fall and Zebulon did not fly in rage at him, he felt calm and strong for having released his thoughts. Maybe this is what being a man feels like, he thought.

The General took a deep breath and calmed himself.

"You are correct but your point holds no relevance in this matter. Out here, as I told you before, there are but two races. White and red. The crimes committed against the Negro back east do not excuse the savage warfare attributed by the savage Indian."

Charles spoke up, perhaps emboldened by the boy.

117

"Whites and Indians been fighting for as long as anyone can remember. If someone came to your house and said, "It's mine now,' would you put up a fight?"

"Poor Charles, at least a quarter of the blood running through you contains savagery. I understand your affinity for them. You see, the purpose of civilization is to rob man of his baser instincts and refine him in such a way that he is capable of functioning in a society. The Indian, having chosen to forgo the transformations that civilization brings, has thus degraded himself into barbarism. Whites fight out of necessity, while the Indian, for fun and what appears to be pleasure. The toll they enacted is nothing more than robbery, committed by a heathen race."

"That toll," Charles began, "is payment for all the land taken by the government. It is nothing compared to the toll they should be taking."

"Charles, I am a fair man and would even concede to your point but my experiences and views on the Indian race and their character . . . differ."

The next morning the canoes were completed, and they crossed the North Platte River. They continued north, and two days later they camped next to a beautiful, tranquil stream. Polar water rushed downward from some of the lower mountains. The early morning sun started its slow warming. The men basked in its comfort as they ate breakfast, engaged in idle chatter. The birds seemed to almost compete with them in volume as they screamed and chirped at one another to no end. Steam whirled upward from the boy's coffee. He had grown to like the drink, especially on chilly mornings such as this.

Over the sound of the rushing stream, the men heard a yell from a voice that did not seem familiar to any of them. The boy dropped his cup in shock, and the men ran over to the voice with rifles in hand.

When they arrived, a large, eight-hundred-pound monster of a grizzly stood over Grunt and made him look like a child. The men dropped their rifles and immediately scurried up the trees. They moved so quickly that they themselves might have had claws on their hands. From fifteen or twenty feet in the air, the men screamed at the boy. The beast was coming closer to him, growling and snarling the entire way.

It takes great bravery to stand your ground while one of nature's deadliest creatures advances toward you. Very few men would ever do so. However, this was not the case in why the boy remained unmoved. Fear bundled his limbs together when the bear showed its razor-sharp teeth. It let loose a low-pitched growl that rattled him to his core. Each step the brute took left paw prints that were sixteen inches long from heel to toe. The boy's heart kicked and punched against the inside of his chest. Being the only thing in his body that moved, it attempted to scamper up the trees with the rest of the company.

Now only fifteen feet separated the boy from certain doom. He broke the paralysis spell just enough to raise his rifle toward it but could not bring himself to pull the trigger. His arms vibrated on their own accord and the rifle attempted to jump out of his hands. His terror only compounded when the bear began to rise on its hind legs. It rose and it did not stop until all nine feet of the animal were now in the air and cast an enormous shadow over the boy. The bear growled again and turned the boy's legs into jelly as he began to drop to the ground.

A loud bang was heard, and the behemoth crashed to the ground in front of the boy with a loud thud. The force of the shot caused the boy's rifle to jump out of his hands. He and the rifle plopped harmlessly to the ground as the smoke still lingered in the air. The company hung in the trees like fruit. They began to cry out and sing the boy's praises once they saw the bear was truly dead. He didn't shoot the bear on purpose. He had just been so terrified that he pulled the trigger by accident and just so happened to be aiming at the animal's heart. One well-placed shot brought the Goliath to its end. Its eyes were still open and stared at the boy while large volumes of blood began to seep out from underneath it.

The company descended from the trees and split up, some checking on the boy and the others checking on Grunt. When the boy regained his composure, he joined the large crowd that surrounded Grunt. It was a wonder that he was still alive. When the bear first sprang upon him, Grunt had dropped his rifle and fought the grizzly hand to hand. His wounds showed the price of such a brawl.

Long, deep gashes where five-inch claws ripped his flesh and muscles were found everywhere on his body. Volumes of blood ejected from them. On his head was a bloody section where a piece of his scalp once sat. He had used his left arm as a shield, which likely had saved his life. The nerve damage was so great that he would never use it at full strength again. With all these injuries, he still managed to let loose a grunt when the distraught General asked if he was okay. Through great pain and strife, eight men were able to lift the massive man and place his body in a clearing. Some of the half-bloods began to patch his wounds to the best of their ability. The General bit his nails and watched the very medicine that he had denounced save the man closest to him.

Two days passed, and Grunt still lay staring up at the sky and could not walk, nor did he open his mouth once to announce discomfort or pain. Roger pulled the General and Charles off to the side, and the three men deliberated for a moment. At first, the General appeared to take offense at what Roger said. He stepped away from the two men in dramatic fashion but returned and reluctantly relented. He called the company together and with a somber face, he spoke.

"The tragedy that has befallen our beloved member Grunt is one that has hurt us all. While we are more than assured that he will recover, we can't afford to hold the expedition for this. It has been decided that we shall continue onward and trap in the Black Hills before heading to the Green River Valley. As for our fallen friend, a volunteer is needed to stay behind with him while he mends and catches up to the group."

Not one hand rose. During the entire journey, Grunt had stood by the General and had not said one word since they had left St. Louis. He did not make jokes, join in on the tricks they played, or tell stories at the campfire. Nothing. He just was there, performing whatever duty the General asked of him. The boy did not feel a connection to Grunt. In fact, had he gone under at the hands of the bear, his presence would have only been missed physically. The sadness in Grunt's eyes compelled the boy to raise his hand. He appeared to be some caring hero, putting others before himself. This was far from the truth, though. He raised his hand more to prove to himself that he held onto bits of humanity. The General's face stretched into a wide smile as he announced their departure in the morning.

The next morning, the company began to take off, continuing in a north, northeast direction. While the pack train moved on, the General stayed behind and spoke to the boy.

"Somehow, son, I knew you would be the one to volunteer."

"No one else would do it," the boy remarked. He now

regretted his decision and showed a bit of an attitude toward it.

"Because they aren't you."

The boy did not respond.

"Grunt means very much to me. Please protect him with your life. But if he does not recover, put him out of his misery. He's a man of the wild and feeling trapped in his body would be a fate worse than death." He handed the boy a small one-shot pistol. "We shall make our trail easy to follow. Godspeed."

The General walked over to Grunt, who lay on two blankets and leaned down on one knee. He spoke words that only the two of them could hear and he held the man's hand tightly. Grunt stared up at him but did not speak, he simply nodded. The General rose and saluted his friend, mounted his horse, and soon caught up with the company. Now the boy and Grunt were alone by the creek.

Some vegetation rustled in the wind, and the boy jumped, thinking about the Sioux. He envisioned them coming back to extract more from the company. What if they returned, scalped him and Grunt, and he was never heard from again? His heart thumped at all the possibilities. He cursed himself for doing this for a man whom he had never even spoken to, whose name he did not even know. But then he told himself that he was doing well by thinking about the wants and needs of Grunt, and this made him feel better. He stared at the man whose gaze remained fixed on the sky.

Night came. The rushing water and the popping crackles of the fire were not enough to drown out the eerie footsteps of the wolves that stalked about. They circled the perimeter of the fire just outside its light. The boy's rifle was firmly rooted in his right hand while a six-inch-long knife sat in his opposite.

He sat across the fire from Grunt. The man was on his back

and looked up at the night sky. The dark void was overcrowded with stars that floated some unfathomable distance away. His beard covered his mouth, and his long brown hair was lying in every direction under the kerchief that sat over his wound. To calm his fears, the boy decided it was better to speak to the man, even if he couldn't speak back.

"I've always wondered what your name was. I'm almost certain it isn't Grunt."

Grunt's eyes popped open. His mouth began to quiver and opened.

"Norman. Norman McCall," he said.

The boy had continued talking and then stopped when he heard him. "What?" His mouth was wide open in disbelief.

"My name is Norman McCall." His tenor voice was scratchy and weak, and he sounded as though he could use some water.

"You can talk? Why haven't you said something before? At least your name?"

"No one ever asked."

"I figured that you couldn't speak at all. You didn't correct Zebulon when he introduced you."

"Zebulon? That always made me laugh."

"Why's that?"

"It ain't his real name."

9

Every Man Has His Limits

"He was born Fred Davis in western North Carolina, named after his paw. He was a lad, maybe eight or nine, and had been away playing with a friend. When he came back home, he found his family all dead. His ma, paw, three little sisters, and older brother, were all scalped and bloody, hacked to pieces by them Indins. This manner is common now and even more back then, when this country was younger. I'm sure you watch how he handles with them Indins and his hate for them."

The boy sat in a ball of confusion and stared at Grunt through wide eyes. The man was gazing up at the sky as he spoke, and the orange glow of the fire lit the right side of his bearded face.

"I had noticed, but it's not strange to hear a white man speak ill of the Indins," said the boy.

"Yea, but his runs deeper than most. He puts up with them out here 'cause we need them to survive, but he would rather they all be put up under."

"His entire family dead? And he's the one that found them? I can't begin to imagine."

"They deaths made him different. His paw went under with no one knowing his name, dead and gone without a trail left behind. That's what motivates the General. His main ambition is for men all over the world to not only know his name but to respect it. He don't wanna die like his paw."

"So that's why he changed his name? To escape his father?"

"He changed his name 'cause Fred Davis sounded too 'normal.' Argan Zebulon is a name that people won't forget. Even the way he acts, he created it to become a figure that people will remember. He refuses to die and no one knows it."

"Is he even a General?"

"Yes. He was a brigadier general in the War of 1812, that part's true. He made a big reputation for being extremely cruel and mean to the Brits and Indins, especially."

"That don't surprise me. How do you know so much about him?"

Grunt turned his head and looked over at the boy. He winced as he struggled to sit up, and soon he towered over the fire. His bones cracked as he twisted his body and neck. He examined his wounds and removed the kerchief from his head. He touched the missing piece of scalp, examined his finger and then placed the kerchief back on.

"I was raised up in Ohio. I always been a big son of a bitch, and when I was a boy, I was fat and slow. Them other kids was mean to me, said I was dumb and all, but really I was smarter than all 'em. But, anyway, I was always close-knit with my family, always and only felt comfortable around them. Well, when I was ten years old, I, too, came home and saw that my lovin' family had been massacred by Indins. I was a lil chap and didn't know what to do, so I stayed. A child don't wanna accept that he's all alone in the world, so I lived with their hacked-up bodies for a month and spoke to them, laughed with them, sobbed with them until the General came across my home, lookin' for a place to stay the night. I was scared and didn't talk to him, he still don't know my name, but he took me with him. Said that ain't no way for a child to be livin,' and he's watched over me and cared for me ever since."

"Do you hate the Indins, too?"

"I hate them that did it but not them all. They ain't done no worse than any white man. 'Sides, ain't no use in hatin' them, I dunno where they are, and it won't bring my family back."

"Why'd you go all them years without talkin'?"

"When you as big as I am, folks think you ain't nothin' more than a monster. Plus I rather be out in the wilderness and was never too comfortable around folk that ain't kin to me. You attach yourself to them, and then they dead and gone."

"But not the General?"

"Not the General. I'd still be livin' with them dead bodies if it weren't for him. So I protect him with my life and won't let nothin' happen to him. He the only family I have left, and we been through the same. So even though I don't talk to him, he understands me and don't need me to."

"Those are two tragic stories," the boy said.

"Yea, but worry more for him than me. We both dealt with our grief in different ways. Me by avoidin' folks and him by attemptin' to have as many folks around as possible. He don't worry or plan 'bout nothin,' and I reckon it'll cause us all to go up under."

"You think so?"

"He ain't all there up here," he said pointing to his skull. "He think it's all about who know your name and ain't figured what matters in life."

"And what's that?"

"Your kin, or the folks you call your kin. We prime examples of what lack of family can do to a man. He been searchin' for it but just don't know it, and I been avoidin' it. We two sides of the same coin, me and him."

The boy didn't make a sound.

"What's so good about not talkin' for years is that you do more listenin' and thinkin.' I come to many understandin's on life." Again he began to move his body around and twist.

"So what are you talkin' to me for?"

"Really? I dunno. You the first person to ask my name in years. The General asked, but I was too scared to say it then. He just started callin' me Grunt, and everyone did the same. I guess in a way, you askin' made me feel like you cared."

Grunt held up his left hand to the fire and inspected where the claw had separated his flesh.

"That son of a bitch really did a number on me. Will you do me a favor?" he asked the boy.

"I done saved your life already, what else you want?" The boy had been making a necklace out of the bear's claws. He laughed and looked up at him.

"Let's keep this between us."

The boy nodded and went back to his necklace.

Two days later, the two started on the trail, and four days later, they caught up with the company. They were making their way toward the Black Hills, taking no heed to the warning from the Sioux. They trekked over an immense wide-open country that rose and fell in gradual sections. They came to one of the hills and looked out, seeing fifty miles in each direction. The snow had melted, and the hills were a wonderful dark-green color, with the trees being half dressed. In the distance sat the tree-covered Black Hills, called that from their dark appearance from afar. Each day the sun lingered in the sky just a little bit longer than it had the preceding day, allowing the men to cover more ground. One evening, the boy was busy setting up camp when the yell of "Indins!" came out, and, like clockwork, the company grabbed their weapons and formed a line.

A small group of six Native men rode up to the company with their hands held high above their heads. They spoke in broken Spanish to the company, who took this to mean they were acquainted with Europeans and therefore friendly. The leader was draped in a robe and wore dark-brown leggings that reached the middle of his thighs. Charles stepped forward and concluded they were Arapaho. He told the General that he knew very little of their language and commenced to speaking in signs. They went back and forth until the Arapaho leader went back to his packhorse and grabbed a pack of beaver fur. He walked back over to the company and tossed it to the ground with a look of satisfaction on his face. Charles put his hands up and looked out at the open land before them, as if to ask where. With a long bony finger, the leader pointed toward the Black Hills and indicated what they took to mean that there were many beaver there. Charles turned to the General.

"What do you think?"

The General looked over the very Natives he had been warned about by the Sioux. Some dressed in the tattered remains of western clothes, previously worn by other mountain men whose fates could only be speculated. They wore coats made of deer and elk hide with round hats made of beaver fur that sat over long, dark locks of shiny hair. Each man was small and thin, their movements quick and shifty.

"We have to play along for the time being, but you all stay on alert."

Charles motioned for the Arapaho to join the camp. Soon they gathered wood for the fire and continued to help with all the tasks of setting up camp. Night came, and soon Carl woke up the boy for his turn at the night watch. The air was cold and crisp, but the boy thought how nothing could be worse than what they experienced weeks before. He sat on a rock with his rifle in his hand. He blew his breath, watching it twist and turn every which way before dissipating into the dark of the night. Roger, Sammy No Scalp, and a Virginian named Thomas King were also on watch and were all similarly engaged.

Save the occasional gust of wind, the night was ghost quiet and altogether peaceful. The moon soared high in the sky and gave the earth a dark-blue tint. This tint grew darker as a large formation of clouds rolled in and completely blocked out the moonlight. Several dozen Arapaho warriors, all terrifyingly painted and armed, arose from under a veil of darkness and emerged from the trees. Fastened under their moccasins were the severed paws of grizzly and black bears. With these, they were silent as they crept up the small hill to the unsuspecting company. They stood but a few yards from the campsite.

The General had been too disturbed to fall asleep. The entire night, his eyes remained fixed on the Arapaho leader. The man's every movement was recorded and studied in the General's mind. The man slept on his side and faced one of his men who also lay similarly. When he made the slightest nod of his head, the General popped up like a man risen from the dead. He leveled his weapon and fired, striking the man in the breast. The blast woke the company, and if it hadn't, a shrilling war whoop would have. The screams echoed from every direction and let the company know that they were surrounded.

The company wasted no time grabbing their rifles. They aimed and fired at sounds, with nothing being visible. The boy trained his weapon at a sound and waited. Within seconds, the nightmarish outline of a ghostly specter materialized. The warrior rose up out of the dark like a summoned demonic creature. The boy took a shot and hit the man on his naked torso. The boy ran over to the man, who now groaned on the ground.

Small slivers of moonlight returned their eyesight. The boy's first instinct was to unsheathe his knife and run it across the man's throat. He snapped out of his violent trance and pounded the butt of his rifle against the man's temple, knocking him out cold.

Sounds of war clashed and erupted for a little under two minutes. When the battle was over and the quiet of night crept back in, the men called out to one another, trying to account for their number.

One casualty belonged to a French-Indian named Étienne Couture. He lay on his back with an arrow sticking out of his neck. Another was a British born man that had a tomahawk lodged in the middle of his forehead. The final hit the boy closer to home.

The young Frenchman Jacques was stiff on the ground with a hatchet to his neck. The boy knelt down at his side and clutched onto Jacques's hand. He looked into the man's brown eyes and watched his soul leave him. His grip on the boy's hand lessened until his entire body had gone limp.

Several of the company were hunched over, extracting their trophies. Zebulon screamed at the top of his lungs, cursing any and everything "Indin." He grabbed a hatchet and hacked and butchered away at the body of one of the Arapaho. The boy walked over to him, and when he saw the mangled and dismantled body, he ran away, throwing up in disgust. A scream just as horrifying caught everyone's attention. Bradan stood next to a tent and frantically looked around while yelling at the top of his lungs.

"Sammy! Sammy!"

The men set out in groups and searched the area for the man. They descended down the hill toward the tree line and tripped over rocks and stones in the near dark. The boy came across his body some fifty feet out of the camp. He knelt down and shook his body after Sammy said something incoherent. The boy called out to the rest of the men, and Bradan ran full speed over toward him and pushed the boy out of the way. He yelled at Sammy and slapped him until Sammy's eyes shot back to life. Bradan pulled the man close and tight, cradling him in his arms like a child and kissing him on the cheek. With an almost paternal instinct, he examined his head and saw nothing out of the ordinary, save his pants being down to his ankles. He had gone off to urinate in the night. When the battle erupted, Sammy was so terrified that he had passed out.

It was too dark to begin to move, so they fortified themselves and waited for retaliation that would not come. When day began to break on the horizon, the three dead men were eulogized by Henry and buried. The company shed quick tears for the men but wasted no time and moved forward toward the Black Hills. The General rode stone-faced and would remain in this way for several days. Behind him were more whispers of his foolishness.

One day, they camped alongside a small stream that was surrounded by lush, green grass on either side. The boy and Roy lay flat on their stomachs on a bluff overlooking one side of the stream. Long cigars hung out of their mouths. With rifles in hand, they watched a few buffalo that grazed about a half mile from the camp.

"C'mon, pup. At least make it a fair bet. I once shot a movin' antelope from over a mile away," said Roy.

"Bull, Roy," the boy said.

"Oh? I'll show ye. And I get one shot?"

"One shot."

"Make it three pairs of mocs."

"All right, fair."

The two shook on the bet, and Roy rose to one knee and put his rifle up to his shoulder and took aim. The buffalo ate slowly and deliberately and did not move at all, making this an easy shot. Roy breathed deeply, then exhaled and held his breath, and then fired. The ball missed the head, and the wounded animal began to scream and run toward camp. Roy cursed once it made it to the camp and began to jump and kick its hind legs every which way. It tossed its head into the General's tent and blinded itself. Having increased its agitation, it knocked pots, pans, saddles, weapons, and packs of fur everywhere. The company again took to the trees for safety and allowed the beast to ravage the camp. It came close to the stream and kicked its way into the water, and just like that was carried along the flow.

"God damn son-of-a-bitch rifle ain't no damn good," Roy barked.

"Yeah, yeah," the boy mocked. "Let me show you how."

Faint screams from the company reached the boy and Roy as they were cursed for their carelessness. The boy paid this no mind, took aim at a large buffalo that was three hundred yards away, and fired. He no longer handled his weapon like a novice but instead seemed rather comfortable with it. Roy would have been proud had he not choked on the smoke from the shot. The buffalo fell while the boy rose and gloated with a little dance.

Beneath them, a young calf ran along the stream, followed the now-drowned buffalo, and called out to it. James crept up close behind it, trying to silently close in on it. He wormed up to it and jumped on its back and seized hold of its neck and attempted to wrestle it down to the ground. The calf was stronger than he thought it would be, and being angered by the death of its mother, it gave a spirited effort and tossed James from its back. Each time James attempted to rise, he was met with a strong head butt to his chest that knocked him back over onto the ground. This comical display continued seven times until he was able to seize the calf by the leg and stab it with his knife. The calf screamed and departed, leaving a trail of blood that James followed onto some vegetation. Ten minutes later, James returned back to the camp, dragging the calf by the legs, its tongue hanging out of its mouth.

The company called out to him, joking and jeering. Roger proclaimed that he was a "the biggest flash in a pan that this old coon ever did see." The boy was flat on his back with his hand over his stomach and laughed from the pit of his soul. Large tears raced from his eyes, and he rubbed them red at he stared up at the pale-blue sky. He had not laughed this hard in months and the release it provided him made him feel that at that very moment, the world was perfect and all was well. He looked over at Roy, who laughed just as hard, and wondered how a sixteen-year-old Roy would have fared in a fight with his father at sixteen.

At night, although it was chilly, the air was clean and fresh and brought joy and renewed the company's spirits. They ate large strips of buffalo meat and, afterward, reclined on the magnificent grass with their pipes lit. They spoke idly on what each would do if he suddenly became a rich man.

"Beyond a doubt, I'd move on up north, New York more than likely," said Henry. "Just to get away from all the craziness. I'd open my own church and spread the Lord's word."

"I hate to be the one to relay this to ye, but you wouldn't be much more welcome in the north, either," said Bradan.

"Are you from New York?" Henry asked him.

"Boston. The northerns don't want Negroes in chains, but they also don't want 'em livin' right next to them, and I'm not too proud to admit but a few months ago, I was one of 'em."

Henry sat quiet for a moment. The boy nodded his head in agreement. Even though he had never been that far north, he had heard some of his father's friends say such things. This notion caused many of the few free blacks to stay in the south even after a few had gained their independence.

"What about you, No Scalp?" Henry asked.

"Huh?" said the bald man, half listening.

"If you suddenly became a rich man, what would you do?"

"He'd open an orphanage," Bradan said.

"Can the lad speak on his own account?" Roger said.

"Of course, but I know what he wants, maybe even more'n he do."

"What's your story, anyway? Ye seem more of a father than his brother."

"In a way, I am. Ma and Paw went under back when we was just wee boys and left us to grow in an orphanage in Boston. The nastiest place ye ever wanted to see, the adults weren't much better. Sammy always been scared, you see, so it was on me to protect him, and after Ma and Paw passed, I had no choice."

"How'd you come to St. Louis?" asked the General.

"We spent some time as criminals. Another thing I ain't too proud to tell, but we did what we had to for survival. Con men, robberies and such, and built up a good sum of money. Ain't any of you the law?"

"Not out here at least," smiled the General.

"We was in a gamblin' hall in Boston. The kind with all types of folk from all walks of life that you would wanna avoid. Well, we were gamblin' with this businessman, real smart-lookin' fella. He had some money on him, that's for sure, and I made a stupid choice that changed both our lives. I took all the money me and me brother had and thought I could win all of his. I bet it all and, just like that, there goes horse and beaver. I lost everything, and I didn't know what to do, but I knew I needed me money back and . . ."

Here he stopped and swallowed hard. Carl stared at Bradan as he spoke. His mouth was open, and he was shaking.

"We robbed him, and the bastard fought back, so we beat him, bad. Left him all broken and bloody. He left me with no choice. Well, it turned out he was some high up businessman, and it didn't take long for word to get out on what we made of him. Me brother was there and naturally helped me, but it was all me. I dragged him into this mess, so it's me job to keep him out of trouble, no matter who it comes from."

Carl stared at the fire.

"When abouts was this?" he asked. The tone of optimism that his voice generally carried was now gone and had been replaced with a low, whispering sound of dejection. In fact, if the boy didn't see it himself, he would not have believed that Carl had been speaking.

"Ahh, five years now?"

The boy switched his gaze from Bradan to Carl when Carl did not respond. A horrified look was etched in stone on his face. A single tear fled his right eye. The boy still didn't understand the significance of Bradan's story.

Carl was typically happy, smiling bright all day, through the downpours of rain, snow, sleet, and arrows. He stood tall and strong and faced every situation with a laugh. Nothing seemed to be able to upset the man or ruin his mood but, as Roger said, "every man has his limits." Carl leaped through the fire and landed on top of Bradan with his hands clenched tightly around the man's throat, cutting off all air.

"That man you beat and robbed and left in the gutter . . . He died . . . You son of a bitch!" he said.

Sammy jumped to his brother's defense, lunged at Carl shoulder-first, and knocked him to the ground. He grabbed his knife and attempted to stab Carl, and had the General not hit his right arm, the knife would have been driven into Carl's eye. Grunt grabbed Carl and all three were raised to their feet, where General Zebulon stood between them.

"Carl, how can you be so sure that they are the culprits?"

The boy watched Zebulon through different eyes after his conversation with Grunt. He could now see that Zebulon enjoyed dramatic moments such as this. In these times, he could interject for his own benefit. He used moments like this as another opportunity to showcase another aspect of his eccentric personality or wisdom.

"They did it," Carl yelled, foaming at the mouth. Dark-red anger and hatred filled his eyes, and when they had reached their capacity, they began to pour out in the form of tears. "Don't worry about your scalp, I'll rip your goddamn head off!"

"It ain't worth it, Carl," the boy yelled, not truly believing that statement.

"You ran away from your family. Mine was taken," Carl said, and the boy remained quiet.

"Carl, we're sorry. This was years prior, and while I wish like hell I could take it back, there ain't nothin' I can do but repent for it!" said Bradan through a badly busted lip.

Grunt held Carl tight against his large body and tightened his grip the more excited Carl became. The two battled each other, and when the force of the hug became too much, Carl conceded. He slid down to the ground, as did tears from his eyes. Defeated and broken, he sat and hung his head between his knees. The General walked over to him and placed a hand on his broad shoulders.

"Carl, your feelings are justified, but this occurred prior to the formation of this party. Any retaliation will lead to your arrest and loss of employment."

"I just found the sons of bitches who killed the man that was closest to me. You think I give a damn about employment?"

"There is no need for me to describe the course of action if you retaliate . . . I got it," the General exclaimed. "You three sit down and I shall mediate a . . ."

"Argan," said Roger. "I reckon you best sit this one out."

Carl said nothing and sat there, looking up at the two men who stared back at him. Carl's face was evil and brooding, and he looked to have been plotting what couldn't have been anything other than revenge. His gaze rarely ever left Sammy or Bradan all that night, and even the next day as they continued their northward travel. The boy pulled his horse alongside Carl and attempted to speak to him but found no luck. The two men that Carl had become close to, one of whom had shot him in the leg and received instant forgiveness, just admitted to the death of his father and this was too much for him, or any man, to take.

Days later, the boy was engaged in trapping another stream. He had picked up four traps, all of which contained beaver. He thought about Henry the beaver and wondered where he was and how he was getting along. Life had to be harder without one of his legs, but then it again, it would be harder if he were dead.

These thoughts were interrupted by the eruption of rifles, some quarter of a mile away. The boy dropped the beaver and ran toward the sounds and arrived to find four dead Natives. The scalps of these men were unlike others. Their hair was the longest the boy had ever seen. One of their locks was more than four feet long. The company hurled their bodies into a pile much like firewood. They stripped the men of everything except their loincloths and placed all of their belongings into knapsacks.

"What happened?" the boy asked.

"We were fired upon and returned the favor," said Zebulon with a devilish smirk on his face.

The next day, the General called the boy to come with him up to a hill to survey the country. As they rode, he wondered just what the General wanted to speak to him about and why. He now felt somewhat awkward around the General. Grunt rode a few paces behind the General. The secret between Grunt and the boy began to weigh heavy on him. He knew so much about the man and his past and was afraid he would let the information slip.

They reached the top of a small mountain, or rather a large hill. An endless sea of grass sat below them. Soon the entire area would be a vibrant green due to the fair amount of snow that winter. The General looked to the northwest and called the boy over to him. The General took a long dramatic pause, and the boy watched him awkwardly.

"Do you think I am a madman?"

"Huh?" the boy said.

"I can hear the rumblings around the camp that I'm leading the group straight toward its demise."

"Well, some decisions haven't been the best, but you did save us the other night. If you weren't awake, they might've overrun us."

The General had been somewhat quiet and introspective up until this. He now perked up and smiled.

"You're right! I did, didn't I?"

"But what does it matter? I always thought you didn't pay any mind to what people think?" He stared at the General with disappointment.

This assertion now changed his opinion on a man he looked up to, but this did not matter to the General anymore, who had heard all he needed to hear. He had saved the group, and this was enough for the story he had written in his mind. He now sat up higher in his saddle, with a triumphant posture as he stared out. He reached into his knapsack and pulled out an old brass telescope and began to scan the country.

"I am considering abandoning the Black Hills plan. We have more than enough furs and can make it to the spring rendezvous." He made a noise out of curiosity when the scope reached to the north of them. "It appears we may have some visitors." He handed the telescope to the boy.

"Take a gander at the hill just to the north of us," the General said. "That look to be a party of mounted savages to you?"

"They're a party of mounted something,'" the boy said. He

closed the telescope with the bottom of his palm before handing it back. The General glared at him and opened it again.

"It appears they've spotted us," said the General.

The arrogant and condescending tone that he regularly spoke with began to disappear as more and more mounted figures showed up on the top of the hill and, soon, a line a quarter of a mile long was visible on the ridge. All sat on big, strong horses and all with long scowls plotted across their brown faces. The foremost figure among them was speaking. He pointed in their direction and slapped his horse on its side. He raced at full speed toward the General's position, followed by an endless horde of many more just like them.

10

Don't Hesitate to Shoot

Soon, almost every inch of the hill was covered with horses and their hell-raising riders. Wave after wave of these dangerous riders came from over the crest. A small squadron of women rode among the men and the boys. They were well distributed in the horde, looking more terrifying than their counterparts. The boy estimated that no less than one thousand were present, and this was conservative. Their long hair, spliced up with buffalo fur, flowed in the wind. Some of their locks trailed more than four feet behind them, almost in the face of the rider to the rear. Each was beautifully dressed in various colors and robes. They wore headdresses with eagle feathers that sat around their already dark, war-painted faces. The sound of thousands of jingling beads shot terror through all that heard them. If that wasn't enough, that heinous war whoop would scare any man, no matter how many times he heard it. The boy stared at the General and could see the same concern in his face.

The boy pulled his horse back and rode down the hill, back to their main camp, with yells of what he had seen. They gathered up the men who were off hunting and formed a defensive line, as they done many times before. This time, however, the boy felt different. Previously he was secure in their fortifications and thought they could take on ten thousand men. Now, as he looked around at the rest of the men who shook and stared through wide teary eyes, he felt they were in grave danger. They posted their backs to the creek, and all was quiet for some time.

Faint pats in the distance turned thunderous as the hooves of the horses and war whoops soon became audible over the gusting wind. Countless men, women, and horses charged down the hill. With them were their usual arsenal of rifles, bows, arrows, and lances. Slaughter seemed imminent under the massive numbers of this war party. Even if they were armed with artillery, the company would not have put a dent in the war party. The swarm came within five hundred yards of the company and sent ten riders out to the center of the field between them.

"Don't hesitate to shoot," the General told the men. "They'll kill us either way."

He and Roger, Roy, Grunt, and Charles all rode out to speak with the warriors. The horses of the war party were just as bloodthirsty as the riders. They were large and looked terrible. They stomped in placed and snarled at the company's horses.

The boy trained his rifle at one man in particular. He was prepared to knock him from his large black horse should it be necessary. The man's hair flowed down past the stomach of his horse. His headdress was decorated with eagle feathers and the tails of brown weasels. Beads hung from his sturdy neck and more were on his well-toned arms. His name was Cut Belly, and his face wore a look of nobility, suggesting dignity and class. This man spoke to Charles with subtle and regal movements.

Behind him, young, war-hungry braves sat restlessly on their mounts. They all were eager to prove themselves as fighters. Cut Belly made a motion to the company, upon which the General looked back and shook his head.

They spoke for about ten minutes until the General rode back to the company. The company relaxed their weapons and exhaled deeply when they saw that the General did not appear worried.

They were of the Crow Nation and were on the warpath against the Arapahos. When Charles informed them of the company's slaughter of a group of the Arapaho, Cut Belly smiled. He invited the company to spend time in Crow country to trap, trade, and hunt, upon which the General readily accepted. Cut Belly offered them a guide, and for three days they rode until they came to the main Crow village.

A hilltop offered a painted view of large, white tipis and the beautiful grassland they dotted. The boy told James that this looked to have been painted by Michelangelo himself, to which James replied, "Who the devil is that?"

As they rode in toward the village, they were welcomed and treated as heroes. Young children ran alongside their horses, and the women brought out gifts of moccasins, shirts, robes, and other items for trade.

One day, the boy slowly walked among the trees with his rifle at ready. In front of him tiptoed Old Roy and to his rear was James. Each wore new moccasins that provided footsteps that were nearly undetectable by human ears. Roy spoke to the boy a bit above a whisper.

"The General has taken a likin' to you."

"He just likes talkin,' and I'm the main one that listens."

"You really think that's the full of it?"

"Well, yeah, what else could it be?"

"These old eyes have seen many winters and I've known men like Zebulon often. His type do everything possible to find glory and be remembered. They change everything about themselves, thinking that's what it takes. They don't know that it come from within. Then there are men who are born to make somethin' of themselves and would do so even if they attempted to stop it themselves. You one of them, pup. I know it, and you best believe the General knows it."

"But how can I when I haven't done anything worth while?"

"Right now, you just figurin' it all out. The best way to learn to hunt is to hunt. You learnin' to hunt right now, and if you lookin' for you to be perfect to be a great man, that ain't gone ever pass. Even the most wisest man makes mistakes often but hear me, pup, you ain't gonna grow to be no regular man. Let the Lord use you, you might like what He does."

"But I don't see or feel like it."

"Strange thing, ain't it, how the world sees somethin' in us that we don't see in ourselves."

James looked confused as if the two spoke in code.

"But if I'm gonna be so great, shouldn't I know it?"

Roy did not respond and threw up his hand to mean silence as he crouched down to one knee. He motioned toward some bushes, and the trio took cover behind them. With rifles at ready, they sat silent and waited for whatever came their way. Indistinct chatter that at first sounded neither English nor Native became clearer. When full English sentences were heard from about fifty yards away, they relaxed.

James, incited by Roy's proclamation over the boy, sought to prove himself just as great. He stood up and jumped out of the bush, intending to speak to the group before Roy or the boy could.

The lead ball tore its way into his shoulder, and the force knocked him down to the ground. The boy and Roy emerged from the bush and rushed to his side. When they emerged, the crack of another rifle went off and almost hit Roy.

"Aw, hell," said the distraught first shooter. He ripped off his grizzly-fur hat and dropped down to examine James. "What in the hell are you boys doin' in the bush like some goddamn Injuns?"

"They worser than Injuns, Sherm," said the man who fired the second shot. He coldly stared at Roy and the boy.

"We're with a company of fur trappers, General Zebulon's group," said Roy as he propped James up and examined the wound. James winced and gritted his teeth at the lead ball that was lodged in his shoulder.

"Wagh! Well, that beats all! He ain't pained too bad, our camp ain't too far from here. We'll get that there ball out," said the first shooter. His accomplice continued to stare down Roy, and the boy who paid him no mind.

The men's names were Sherman and Thomas. They were a part of a group of free trappers who had claimed to have been in the wild for more than four years now. Everything about the men supported this claim. They were dressed in the hide of dead animals and wore moccasins that were as filthy as their wild hair. Long beards covered their aged faces.

Their camp was small and pitiful and hardly worth the five-mile walk, except for James being well taken care of. Later that night, they sat around a fire with five other men and ate a dinner purely of buffalo meat. The subject started off on the Natives.

"They the most brutal sonbitches this hoss ever had the displeasure of comin' across," said Sherman.

"Especially them damn Blackfeet," said a man named Jack.

"Blackfeet? We haven't come across them yet," the boy said.

"You remain around these parts much longer, and you will. We took you for them, that's why you were shot at so mighty quick. They cruel sonbitches, that's for sure . . . You said you all are with Zebulon's outfit?"

"Yes."

"Wagh! Beats me how you all made it this far," said Sherman.

The group's laughter made the boy feel uncomfortable and somewhat embarrassed.

"I best be careful what I say, 'fore you run and tell the General what old Sherman been saying. I know one thing for certain, Zebulon with all his war glory still can't hold a torch to them Blackfeet. All Injuns are mean bastards, but they the only kind that will kill a whole village, even women with child, as they would warriors."

"They that bad?" the boy asked.

"They even worse'n that. A pal of mine knew a man, his name was, uhh George Dempsey, that was him, who had gone to the Upper Missouri in the early days of the fur business. He got himself captured by the Blackfeet, who hate white men more than white men hate them. They burned him alive and fed him to they pet dogs, and whatever was left of the body, they wear to this day as necklaces."

The other men shook their heads in collective disgust. The boy didn't believe the exaggeration and changed the subject.

"Well, what do you know about the Crow?" the boy asked.

"The Crow? They fair, as far as Injuns go. The only way a Crow crosses a white man is if the white man crosses him first."

"There's always somethin' worse than a Crow, Blackfoot, any of them," said Thomas.

"What's that?" Sherman asked.

"A nigger." Silence swept through the camp. "I was in charge of a couple myself, down there in Georgia, and they the laziest sonbitches you wanna lay peeps on. Scared of a good day's work."

"Goddamnit, Thomas," cut in Sherman. "Cut all that nigger talk. It's been nice to have some company, and we shot one of theirs, so the least we can do is be goddamn hospitable. I myself have only been able to kill but a few Blackfeet, they the toughest warriors out of all the Injuns, and that's the way my stick floats about that."

"I raised the hair off five of them. You ever killed a man?" Jackson asked the boy with a snide tone. "The first few are the toughest, but after that, it becomes second nature."

"I've sent a few Indins up under. Oh and a couple pale faces that bothered me."

Thomas and the boy exchanged glares for a moment before the subject was changed. Roy laughed at this, and soon he sat on night watch and stared at the boy, watching over him with a paternal eye.

The next day, the trio rode back to their camp with James crudely bandaged up but alive and breathing. After a week had gone by, the company began to become restless. They collected all the beads, shells, knives, pottery, and jewelry that they could carry. Before they could leave, Cut Belly's war party returned with over one hundred and twenty scalps. He convinced them to stay for the scalp dance that was performed that night. The boy watched the Crow dance around the fire that illuminated the dried scalps. He looked over at Sammy. The man's hand was glued to his waist, near his pistol. Bradan placed an arm around him and kissed him on the side of his egg shaped head.

A few days later, the first pink lights of the day plastered on the horizon. The company readied to leave and all sat on their horses, some new, some old. They thanked the Crow for their hospitality that even the General appeared to be at comfort with. Cut Belly stood with his robe covering his half-naked body. He looked to be near to tears as the company rode off to a hero's farewell. The General hoped to make it to the Green River Valley and spend the summer there, and all signs indicated toward a favorable trip. When they stopped for lunch, the boy found the General some fifty yards from the group. He sat on a rock and twirled a bone flute in his hands.

"What'd you think of them Indins?" he asked.

"They are still Indians, but I must admit they were fair, sturdy, and of the utmost character, and if ever I was to put an inkling of trust into a savage, it would be with their kind. But they are still Indians."

After about an hour of riding, Bradan yelled from the back of the pack. The boy turned around, and a large horde of warriors again came dashing toward them. Out front again was Cut Belly, and his mood seemed to have shifted in the few hours the company had been gone.

"Perhaps they mean to warn us of something," the General said. "Stay here, I shall see what this is about. Come, Charles."

They pulled their horses back around to the end of the caravan. They rode out to the open field to meet the warriors. Their number didn't exceed two hundred warriors, and this calmed the company. Carl sat on his horse next to the boy. He appeared to be more anxious than anyone.

The General was rarely seen with no weapon in hand when a Native was around, but such was the case as he rode toward them. By now the Crow had stopped advancing and watched

Charles and the General advance.

The General stopped his horse some fifty feet from Cut Belly, who raised his rifle, leveled it, and fired. The General's body fell off his tall horse and crashed stiff to the ground with a thud. Before anyone could register what happened, Charles, too, received a shot. The lead ball struck him in the forehead, pushing his body backward, leaving his lifeless form to recline against the back of the saddle until it began to slide from the mount. His right foot was caught in the stirrups, and he fell off and was dragged along the ground for some distance until the horse shook him loose.

The company became hysterical. Some dropped from their mounts and took up a fighting position, while others attempted to flee the slaughter. The boy saw Bradan and Sammy each take off toward the west, and soon twelve horses flew passed and chased after them. Rifle smoke filled the air, and men fumbled around and reloaded, all while more Crow closed in. One of the riders took his left leg out of a stirrup and shifted his entire body to the right side of his horse. He continued to ride as such and not once did he look anything but calm. In his right hand was a tomahawk that hung down near the ground. When his target was five feet away, he began his swing and lodged the blade in the stomach of one of the men. By now, many of the Crow had dismounted their horses and galloped around, whooping and screaming while running toward men. They cut off scalps, fingers, and hands. Hacked away at the bodies, nearly bathing in the blood. Those who attempted to flee were chased and shot down like dogs before being mutilated.

After firing a shot, the boy gave up hopes of reloading. With a tomahawk in his right hand, he looked around for his horse in an attempt to flee. Through the veil of dust that surrounded him, it lay fifteen feet away with eleven arrows sticking out its large body. A Crow took aim and fired at the boy. A hard knock hit his left arm, and the boy began to run but to where, he did not know. He jumped and tripped over many of the company who were sprawled out on the ground. Roger was bleeding from the scalp. He looked up from the ground and reached out to the boy, with tears in his eyes. Another arrow jolted his body and permanently closed his eyes. Many of the men were drenched in their own blood, covered with dirt and even their own intestines. Several more marksmen took aim at the boy. When Cut Belly gave the signal, a volley of arrows and lead balls zipped through the air toward him. Grunt emerged and tossed his large frame onto the boy. His enormous body was littered with the projectiles as the boy lay under him. When the gunfire and war whoops ceased, smoke and dust shrouded the ghostly battlefield. Men cried out faintly for their mothers in French and in English, while from others came unintelligible sounds that were followed by death's peaceful silence.

11

A Deadly Game

T he boy's hands were bound behind his back and up against a post. A chord dug deep into his wrists. He could feel the blood in his wrists pumping hard against the restraint. When he opened his eyes, he was inside of a dim tipi, and he stared at a small fire at its center. His breaths became short and quick when he could not remember where he was or how he got there. His left arm was bandaged and throbbed just as bad as his head did.

In his preoccupation, he had not seen Roy and Carl in the tipi with him. Both of them tied up and specially wounded in their own way. Roy and Carl both sat with their heads hung down toward their chests. Both were naked to the waist and were thought to be dead, had the boy not seen their stomachs rising and falling. Soft sobbing came from someone to the boy's left. It was James. He still had his scalp but looked to have received a bullet wound on the left side of his stomach. He had been shot twice within the space of a week, and the reality of the situation was too much to handle. The boy spoke in a voice a little above a whisper.

"James . . . James."

James turned his head over to the boy. His eyes were puffy orbs of red, and his face drooped to the ground, weighed down with depression and hopelessness.

"Where are we?" the boy asked.

"We had no business comin' out here," he said as he rocked his upper body back and forth. "I don't wanna die out here."

"James, get a hold of yourself." The boy paused, surprised that he was handling this so well and keeping his composure. "What happened to all that Indin–killer stuff?"

"It was all a lie, all of it. I didn't have a hard time growing up. My dad is one of the richest men in the city of Richmond. I made all that up, thinking I needed to be tough and that coming out here would be fun. Now, I'm held by savages."

The boy made a mental note of all that and would come back to it later. For now, what mattered was them getting out of this, regrouping with whomever was still alive, and escaping.

"You been up this whole time? When was the last time they came in here?" the boy asked.

"Do you think they'll eat us? I heard that's what even the noblest savages will do."

"James, listen to me. We have to get out of here."

"I wonder what my mom is doing. She was a good gal, she'd lose it if she knew what I got myself into."

"Damn it, James, you not gonna die here if you listen to me."

The boy wasn't sure of this himself. He had no plan, no weapons, and no real knowledge of the territory, but for some reason, confidence shot through his voice as he uttered the words. Perhaps, spurred by nothing more than his own desire to see home once more.

"You know?" said James. "I told my parents I was coming

out to St. Louis to buy land. They think I'm out there some rich man sitting in a brick house with a pretty young wife who will come back to home to meet them. Not tied up half naked in a savage's tent!" His voice began to rise.

"Shut your goddamn mouth or they'll come in here. We need to come up with a plan before they do. They haven't killed us yet, so we got some time."

"There's no use," said Roy. He had woken up a few seconds prior from James's whining. "He's gone in the head. His life is flashing before him, along with his death. Ain't no plan comin' from that one."

"Roy," the boy felt relieved. In Roy, he felt a fatherly protection. Now that Roy was awake, he, if no one else, would know how to escape this situation.

"I ain't gone under yet," he groaned. There was a small nick on his head where an arrow had passed and just missed any critical impact.

"How we gonna get out of this?" the boy asked.

"I'm not so sure, pup." Roy looked over at James, who still rocked back and forth and spoke to himself in a whisper.

"What the hell they attack us for?" the boy asked. "Every-thing was friendly and cordial."

"It could be anything. How long has it been?"

"I don't know, I came to a few minutes ago, and this one ain't no help."

"He alive?" said Roy, referring to Carl.

"Yeah, just out of it."

"I damn sure can use some of that positive mess from him right now. I just remember looking up at the sky and one of them ugly Indin bastards stared down at me. I 'ssume he knocked his rifle on my head 'cause it sure as hell feels like it.

Where's the General?"

"He got shot in front of you as he did me."

"He dead?"

"I assume so."

"And Henry?"

"Took a hatchet to the lungs. If he still kickin' somewhere, he won't be for long," the boy said with a sad look in his eye.

The flap of the tipi was pushed open, and five Crow men bent down and entered. The first two held the flap for Cut Belly, who had to bend more than the rest to enter. He was a large man and despite his muscular frame, his stomach stuck out quite far. He said something to his soldiers and they each went to one member of the company. One of them slapped Carl. He screamed when he stared at the large face that was painted bright red and dark yellow. The Crow man said something in his language regarding Carl, and they all began to laugh. They tied together the feet of the prisoners and then untied their hands and stood them up, with James crying all the while. He would have continued to wail if one of the Crow didn't punch him in the stomach. Their hands were then tied again, and the Crow led them out of the tipi, into the dark of night.

The Crow placed robes over the men to keep them warm from the cool air that bit when it breezed by. They passed by several tipis similar to the one they had just left. Plastered on the outside were crudely drawn pictograms that depicted battles against other tribes, famous buffalo hunts and even their story of creation. They walked by young children who stared at them through wide eyes, partly illuminated by the lights of torches.

A young woman locked eyes with the boy. Her beautiful face called out to him and seemed to empathize with his situation. He turned his head from her and scolded himself for recognizing her beauty in a time such as this. Instead, he began to take note of their surroundings and looked for any possible means of escape.

Behind him, James, with large tears in his eyes, dropped to the ground and refused to walk any farther. The boy strangely felt embarrassed as three Crow men picked him up and carried him like they would a hunted animal. Even the women and children laughed and pointed fingers at his cowardice. James, however, did not seem to notice or care. He screamed out oaths to God and promised that he would never turn his back on his family again. As loud as he was, it appeared that God had turned a deaf ear to him. They came to a circular clearing with a large, raging bonfire in the middle.

Twenty-two poles sat around the fire, all planted into the earth. Waving in the slight breeze were the dried scalps of several men of the company, along with one oddity. A human head, as bald as a stone, sat with its mouth wide open and petrified eyes that stared up at the night sky. Dried blood was caked at the bottom of Sammy's neck. His facial expression showed the horror he had been in prior to his death. The boy turned his head at the sight, then thought that having a scalp for them to take would have been better for him.

They sat some thirty feet from the blaze, the heat keeping them warm on that chilly night. A crowd of men, women, and children, all with eager faces, began to flock to the clearing. After the spectators were all assembled, a group of warriors made their way to the center. The crowd spoke among themselves. The boy didn't need to speak Crow to see that they were all very excited for the festivities. He shook with anxiety. Was this another scalp dance or some kind of Crow killing ceremony?

A man began to howl at the sky, signaling the start of the

dance. The painted warriors began to shuffle and move slowly in a circle, chanting and grunting as they did so. They began to pick up speed and jumped up and down, alternating between leaping off of one leg or two. While in the air, they brought their knees toward their chests. Upon landing, they would emit some loud buffalo growl. They clutched onto lances, knives, and rifles and thrust, spun, and twirled them into the air, simulating battle movements. With scowls on their distorted faces, they looked hideous enough to cause even the bravest men to shake. A young warrior with a deep scar along his left eye jumped toward the boy and thrust his lance at him. The boy readied to spit at the man but a sound from Roy convinced him otherwise. Loud hissing sounds whizzed from the warrior's wide, flared nostrils, and he stared at the boy as the rest of the warriors continued the dance. After about a minute's standoff, he resumed the dance and jumped away from the boy.

A group of women sashayed their way to the center of the ring. They sent the already jubilant crowd into a frenzy as they grabbed the scalps. They held them high in their hands as if they were offering them to God. The warriors increased their jumps and barked out loud into the night sky, putting even the nocturnal beasts on alert. They stomped and stamped both feet into the ground and kicked up a layer of dust that lingered around their kneecaps. They gave loud screams and boasted about the battle, their bravery, the weakness of the enemy, and their grief over their fallen brothers. The dance continued in this way for several minutes until the warriors let out one final, chilling yell. All breathed heavily like bulls and glared toward the company's direction. Roy did not look impressed and actually appeared to nod off at certain moments. Inspired by this lack of concern, the boy did not show that he was shaken to his core. They were led back to the main tipi and fastened to the posts. All that night, they attempted to get some sleep while James's incessant whimpering continued in the background.

A violent shake woke up the boy. Tall and muscular, a long-haired Crow stood over him. Initially, the boy felt empathetic toward the Natives. He even gave indifferent shrugs when white trappers and settlers were killed. However, now that his company was attacked without reason, he, too, began to feel rage toward them. The Crow spoke to his companion in a mocking tone and elicited a response from the boy.

"You untie me and let's see if you're laughin' then," he said.

"Easy, pup," said Roy. "The last thing you want to do is piss them off even more."

"They ain't got no right to slaughter our people and take us prisoner."

"Maybe not. But they have taken us prisoner, and when you caught as a prisoner, you keep your mouth shut and do as they say until you can make an escape. That simple."

They were fed spoonfuls of cornmeal out of a clay bowl and led out of the tipi. They passed a group of women who stopped their morning chores to watch the prisoners. Small children, covered in deer-hide robes ran around the tipis, engaged in a game of hide-and-seek. By now the boy had accepted that his innocent days were gone and he watched them with envy.

Whether he wanted to be or not, he was a man now, and he knew that Roy's words were correct. His actions led him to this place and whether the Crow were to eat him or fill his body with arrows, the fault was his own. This realization strangely put him at peace and gifted him strength, though a feeling of sadness hovered over him. His parents could not see the man he had become, and this hurt him. Then he thought that this was for the best. His hands were now stained with the blood of several men. How could he face his parents as he was?

The Crow put the men on four wild-looking horses. They rode in the middle of a detachment of fifty men, all led by Cut Belly. The tight rope that secured the boy's wrists was tethered to the stone-faced man who woke him up that morning. They rode the entire day and at their night camp, the company sat silent and tethered as they watched the Crow laugh and joke among themselves.

The next day they rode again in similar fashion. Shortly after midday, they stopped at a vast open prairie. At the edge of this prairie sat a dense forest of pine trees with no more than four feet between each tree. The Crow led them down off of their mounts and stood them all in a line, facing the forest. They now began to remove the company's robes, leggings, breechcloths, and moccasins until they were naked as the day they were born.

The boy shivered with his hands over his privates on that chilly day. James stood in the same way, though he shook more out of fear than the temperature. Cut Belly strolled in front of the men and called someone over to him. A short, small Crow man who spoke negligible English came forth and listened to Cut Belly speak. His puzzled face stared into the sky for a moment before he looked at the company and spoke.

"You, fast?" he said while making a running motion.

Almost collectively the company shook their heads in a no fashion, sensing the obvious reason behind this question. Cut Belly spoke to the interpreter and gave a strong laugh.

"You will," smiled the interpreter. "Run trees, you escape."

Roy scoffed.

"They want us to run, and they'll chase us. If we can escape, we can leave."

"What do you think?" asked the boy.

"Don't think we have much of a choice. It's better than havin' your head on a pole while they dance around it."

The boy knew that Roy would rather die fighting than to be taken prisoner and played with. He wondered why Roy would agree to a game with the Crow. Perhaps Roy was only going along with this to protect him, the boy thought.

"They're madmen," said Carl. "I'd rather you kill me right here and now like a man. At least let them go, they had nothing to do with this."

The men looked down the line at Carl with puzzled looks. Before they could say anything, the translator continued his broken instructions. He spoke a little louder to be heard over James's crying.

Behind the company stood a group of young braves. Some with bare chests and others with buckskin shirts, but all looking wild and atrocious. They held bows in one hand and three-foot-long arrows in the other, as well as an assortment of knives, lances, and rifles. They began to hoot and holler in terrible, high-pitched noises that echoed throughout the area. Like wild bulls, they kicked up dirt from the ground and gave loud grunts. Cut Belly stood ten feet in front of them. He looked very pleased at the braves' showmanship as he raised his hand high into the air.

"Don't look back," said Roy. "We gotta stick close to each other. We have more of a chance of survivin' that way." The boy gulped and nodded his head as he looked at James, who he worried for more than the elder Roy.

Cut Belly dropped his hand, gave a whoop, and the company began to race across the field. James stumbled upon pushing off the ground. As a result, he was several steps behind the boy, who led out in front, closely followed by Roy and Carl.

"Don't stop until we reach the forest," Roy yelled.

He had been keeping up with the younger men and was even able to speak while running without losing a breath. Behind them, like a pack of wild dogs, the young braves continued to growl and intimidate, held back by some unseen force as they watched their meal escape before them. They laughed maniacally as they pointed at which member of the company they would kill and placed bets on whose scalp they would raise while they screamed, taunted, and jumped around, eager for their chance to prove themselves to their people.

The company had nearly breached the forest when Cut Belly let loose a siren-like whoop. His group of young braves sprung from where they stood and trampled the ground. They galloped across the field while yelling, screaming, and boasting the entire way. Some of the elder Crows began to fire lead balls and arrows at the company, who was nearing the forest.

"Don't look back," Roy said. His breaths were becoming shorter, and the boy could now hear fatigue in his voice.

The boy slowed his pace and looked back, anyway, allowing Roy and Carl to surpass him. He saw James lying face down until a warrior grabbed him up by the hair and ran his blade across his scalp before running the same blade across his throat. Horror, shock, and regret all blended on James's face, and it would remain so until the critters began to eat away at his skin.

"James," the boy said before he started running again.

He jumped over a fallen branch, and when he landed, a piercing pain shot through his entire right foot, courtesy of a sharp rock that seemed as if it had been placed in that exact spot for this precise moment. He left a bloody footprint with each step, but this annoyance was small in comparison to the branches and twigs that cut and scratched every inch of his body. The bottoms of his feet received the worst treatment, and he grimaced with each step.

The boy caught back up with Carl and Roy, who both also had blood seeping from everywhere on their bodies. He came alongside Roy, who scolded him for slowing down to watch James. From about thirty feet out, a brave screamed and flung his hatchet at them. It made a whooshing noise as it cut through the fresh air. Carl yelped when the blade tore through his skin and lodged itself into the muscles on the left side of his torso. He instantly dropped to the ground, and the brave now began to pull out and level his rifle. The boy dropped to the ground and pulled the hatchet out. Without any thought or aim, he mustered all his strength and threw it back. The throw was dismal, but the hatchet caught the brave in his stomach. By accident, the man discharged his ancient weapon.

Survival instincts kicked in for the boy, and he performed these actions with fluidity and such confidence that had he thought about it, he would have surprised himself. He ran over to the brave, pulled the hatchet out, and ran back to his remaining two company members. Carl clutched at the wound to stop what seemed to be pint after pint of blood from spurting out. Behind him, Roy winced in pain as he looked down at the accidental shot that hit him in his stomach. They held Carl up and began to escape deeper into the forest while the party of terribles still raged after them, stalking and tracking at every turn.

The hard ground now began to slope upward and slowed down their run. The boy's thighs and calves began to curse him in anguish. After half a mile of this uphill climb, Carl's excessive blood loss caused him to collapse to the ground. He crawled over to a tree and leaned his back against it while Roy and the boy stopped to run back toward him.

"You have to get up or they'll kill you," said the boy.

"Let them. I don't deserve to live anymore."

"I don't have the time to argue with you about this, now get up," he barked.

"A goddamn hatchet hit my side! I can't run anymore nor do I want to," he said with a sad look in his eyes as he began to cry. "I'm the cause of all this."

"What? No, you ain't. Somethin' set them Indins off."

"No. I'm dying already so I should come clean. Them four Indins we killed and took their possibles? I put them in Bradan and No Scalp's sacks and showed it so them Crow will see it. I hoped they would only hurt them two, but they attacked us all. This all on my hands," he said, now completely breaking down.

Carl would not look the boy in the eye. His body was slightly hunched over and looked as if he would not live through the night. His right hand sat across his body and covered the wound that still emitted small spurts of blood. The boy gripped the bloody hatchet tightly and also held onto thoughts of driving it into Carl's neck until the yelling of the braves stopped him. Without saying a word, he turned his back on Carl. He and Roy continued their uphill hike and this time, the boy did not look back as the braves scalped the man and delivered the finishing blow.

The pair kept moving, as did the sun, and they lost track of time and how far they had run. The boy stood at the top of a mountain and rubbed his bleeding thighs. Roy arrived several seconds behind him, holding his wounded stomach. His adrenaline had begun to wear off, and he complained about the pain often, which was quite unusual for Roy. At the top of the mountain was a clearing that gave an open view of the surrounding countryside. To the north sat several small hills that had a dark-blue tint due to the coming darkness, while behind them was the dark, ominous forest they had just come from. Almost everywhere on the mountain and the lands below was covered with trees. In the distance, they could hear the branches moving, being parted by the braves.

"Where will we go, Roy?"

"Into the hills," he said pointing to the southeast. His voice lost its strength and, for the first time, the boy began to worry about him. The gentle rolling Black Hills appeared to be endless. "There has to be another trappin' party there."

Slowly and gingerly, the two made their way down the mountain, avoiding stones, sticks, and rocks as they did so. Roy's movements became slower and slower until he asked the boy to stop. The stillness of night brought silence that the two dared not break. They took shelter under some trees that had fallen a few weeks prior and did not move. This time, the boy kept a watch over Roy and woke him occasionally as he did so.

The boy couldn't control his shivering body. He cupped his hands and tried to breathe warm air into them but soon, both they and his feet were all numbed from the cold. What's worse, his heart jumped at every sound of the night, from the soothing hoot of the owl to a howling gust of wind. While these things initially kept him up, his fatigue eventually caught up to him, and soon he shut his eyes and before long, both he and Roy were fast asleep.

When he woke, a light frost covered the forest ground, which was barely illuminated by the soon-to-be-rising sun. He lay flat on his back and for a moment was angry that the sun was taking its sweet time in bringing warmth. He wiggled from under the fallen trees and slowly stood up. He half expecting an arrow to pierce his stomach at any moment, and when it did not, he rubbed his hands up and down his arms to warm them. His fingers passed over what seemed to be hundreds of insect bites that protruded from his skin. His bones were frigid and his arm and feet both troubled him, but he felt strangely optimistic.

The Crow hadn't found him during the night, and he hoped they would give up their chase and leave them be. He and Roy could now escape and would find their way out of this forest and back home to their families. But then he remembered that Roy didn't have a family, and he thought maybe he could bring him home with him. The pain of a rusted nail being driven upward through his feet shot through him with every step he made in an attempt to warm himself. He hobbled back over to where Roy lay, pushed his body, and spoke softly to him.

"Hey, Roy. Roy?"

Roy's eyes were shut, and his hands were gently folded over his wound. They had attempted to clean it as best as they could the night before and little traces of blood still circled it. The boy placed his hands on Roy's frozen body and began to panic. He ferociously rocked him back and forth until the man's big arms and hands fell limp at his side. Despite the icy temperatures and the lead ball lodged in his organs, Old Roy looked to have transitioned to the spiritual realm in relative peace.

12

Alone in the Woods

The boy cried over the corpse of a man whom he had come to see as something of a family member. Old Roy had a fatherly personality. He exuded strength and protection that a family and children need, boys especially. The boy's feelings for Roy were in fact very similar to the feelings he had for his father. Whenever a problem reared its head, he could always go to his father or Roy for an answer, no matter how small. As a child, he had found a dead bird outside. Not knowing what to do with it, he retrieved his father, who did nothing more than bury it. Having a strong figure to navigate minuscule moments such as that are priceless to a child who is trying to make sense out of a chaotic world. The boy now sat cold and alone, inside and out.

For more than thirty minutes, he remained motionless next to the dead man. He would have continued to sit there but for a rustle in the pine needles that caught his attention. A family of deer walked by and snapped him out of his trance, and he realized that he must leave the area.

He remembered the frightening screams from the braves. If

the Crow were still chasing him, they would have woken before he did and would soon find his tracks. He pictured his severed head sitting on a pole while the Crow danced and screamed around it. Immediately, he began to cry and wished he were home.

He grabbed Roy's cold, lifeless hand and thanked him for everything. With teary eyes and a heavy heart, he forced himself to leave the body where it lay and promised that one day, he would return to place a marker for him.

The sun now peeked through trees in this less-dense area of the forest. Its warmth made the temperature more tolerable but his hunger, wounds, and scratched-up body all continued to torment him. Pain jolted through him, as each step was like stepping on large needles that penetrated his feet, up to his knee. He gingerly made his way down a hill and slipped and rolled his ankle as he tumbled to the bottom of it. He cursed under his breath and held onto his ankle and watched it swell up to the size of a sweet potato. He rose and began to delicately place pressure on it, knowing that he must go on.

Branch, stick, stone, prairie-dog den. Repeat. His feet endured all these obstacles for hours on end until night came again. He found himself sleeping under some vegetation that he ripped away from trees. He made no efforts to cover his tracks, and at that point was too cold and tired to care.

The next day, the pain began to become unbearable. His ankle was now twice its normal size and when he rose, he could put no weight on it. He found a branched shaped like a Y with a long tail and bound it together with several other long branches to create a rudimentary crutch for himself. With his right arm on the crutch and his left hand still holding onto the bloody hatchet, he kept moving forward.

He dragged his way through a section of forest that offered no new scenery. His feet were large and swollen, and the pain they were in would often bring him to tears. To distract himself, he began to think as a philosopher would, and he debated many things in his mind. He thought about the Natives he had encountered and how they were just normal humans who wanted their own happiness, even if that meant living in huts, except the Crow, whom he would hate for the remainder of his life. He thought about the freedom he so badly asked for and sarcastically laughed at himself as he was now freer than any black man had ever been on this continent, naked in the wilderness without a white man near him. His mind shifted to Roy's words on how a person's life is in their own hands and how blaming others for your problems is a sign of weakness. He did not want to be weak anymore, and he drilled those words in his head until he could think of them no more.

He thought about the murders he had committed. Already, that part of his soul had begun to cool and harden. He felt nothing about the deaths of the Irishman and the old man on the steamboat. He realized that he had protected himself from men who meant him harm. If need be, he would continue to do so as long as it was his God-given right to defend himself. In fact, a small part of him seemed to enjoy the act. His killings of Natives, however, presented more of a challenge.

He and the company were invading their land. Bill assaulted a daughter of the Kaw. They simply reacted in the same way that any self-respecting group would have done. He felt empathy for the Natives but then shamed himself for having not shared the same empathy for his people. It was wrong of him to look down on those who were forced to be slaves. They were his people, and he promised to God that if He helped him out of this situation, that he would do something to help the cause for abolition, even if it meant losing his life.

He had been so close to death at so many intervals that it did not faze him anymore. The thing that brought him to a shudder was the thought of not living to apologize to his parents. This kept him moving forward through the worst pain he had ever experienced.

His steps began to stumble two days later, as his stomach howled for something more than berries. He came close to killing a wounded deer but did not have the strength to toss the hatchet the twenty-five feet to hit it. On the sixth day, he plodded through the seemingly endless forest, unsure of even which way he was headed. This section of forest became so thick that he was hardly able to bring his body through the trees and vegetation. In this grove in particular, so little light came through the canopy at the top of the trees that though it was now noon, it appeared to be around dusk.

Having lost himself in the forest, he saw what looked to be a clearing up ahead. He quickened to a pace that he did not know he had in him. If he could make it out of the forest, he could find a herd of buffalo and kill one, providing himself with food and clothing. He thought about the nutritious meat and licked his dry lips as he pushed through some trees, eager to run to the herd on the prairie below. What he saw killed his resolve.

There was indeed a clearing, circular shaped and about one hundred yards in diameter. But all around it was more of the dark, impenetrable forest. Twenty yards from him, a small creek babbled. He dropped to his knees and slowly splashed water onto his face and all over his body. His foot was huge, and the cold water that he dipped it in soothed him. He then drank from the stream and its pure, untouched waters refreshed him and slightly alleviated his dizziness. He raised his head, and across the creek, off to his right, sat a cluster of tipis. He wondered how he had missed them before.

He wasn't sure to what tribe these Natives belonged, but he knew from the vibrant colors of the tipis that these were not Crow. He didn't hesitate to walk up to them. He gave out a soft call that no being that walked on four legs could have heard. A ghostlike feeling came over his body. He did his best to tiptoe toward the camp, his thumping heart giving away his position. He was sure of what he wanted to find but not prepared for what he figured he would.

He took his time and surveyed the perimeter of the cluster. Several fire pits sat with still smoldering fires. Holes caused by arrows ruined the beautiful animal-skin tipis. At the entrance of one of these in the back, the boy saw a body lying face down. Flies buzzed on and around the fresh and bloody scalp that was missing a piece. Not far from this body were seven others just like it. All of their throats had been slashed, and one was covered from head to toe in stab wounds from a lance.

At first, the boy was careful not to disturb the deceased bodies but soon began to full-fledge scavenge their clothing. A moccasin was barely able to be pulled over his swollen right ankle. His feet were frozen rocks, and he felt thankful for the little warmth and comfort the moccasins brought him. He took the belt from one of the men and made a breechcloth to cover his genitals. A gunshot-filled buckskin shirt that was too small for him completed his outfit.

The tipis stood unguarded and invited him to rummage through them. In one he found dried strips of buffalo meat. He kneeled over a clay dish and tore at the strips, sneering and snorting. He caught a glimpse of himself in a mirror that sat across the tipi. Crumbs of meat were splattered around his mouth, and he was hunched over like some feral creature. He stopped himself and began to eat in a manner that his mother would find acceptable. Immediately as the meat hit his stomach, he could feel the strength radiate and be redistributed throughout his body.

He remembered not to eat too much after nearly starving, a lesson he learned after being saved by the Pawnee. The scientific reason for this was not clear, but he did know that it worked, and he performed the ritual to be safe. He chuckled at the fact that the Indians, who had no school, often knew more than those who acted as intellectual authorities. The same had been so with his own family. His illiterate grandmother reportedly was able to cure almost any affliction.

He grabbed a knapsack from near the edge of the tipi and placed the remaining strips of meat in it as he left the tipi. He went from tipi to tipi and salvaged anything of use. The final tipi was a beautiful red-and-yellow color. The drawings on it depicted a bloody battleground with the carcasses of many dead horses.

The boy opened the flap and below him lay the lifeless body of a small male child, no older than perhaps five. He was horribly disfigured and had been beaten with a stone club so badly that there were dents all over his body. The boy threw his hands to his eyes, but it was too late. He had already seen the horror, and his stomach had begun to twirl as he turned out of the tipi to throw up.

The mangled face of the innocent child flooded the boy's eyes with tears. When he composed himself, he took the hatchet and began to cut away at the dirt near the stream. He cut away through his hunger pains and dizziness, and an hour later, a four-foot-deep grave was open to the elements.

He found a beautiful red-and-yellow blanket that had a wonderful zigzag pattern sewn onto it and spread it out on the floor of the tipi. It took several attempts before he could gain the strength to pick up the child's body. He set it on the blanket and carefully wrapped the boy. He slowly walked to the grave, ignoring his own pain by focusing on the boy's. He set the body down in the grave and cried like a brother would, as he eulogized the boy's funeral and continually apologized to him as if his hands were stained with his blood. Scoops of dirt began to cover the body. He hoped he placed it deep enough so that the wolves would not make another free meal out of it. Once this was done, anger roused up in him, and the pain he felt himself disappeared.

Just where was God? If "He will not leave you or forsake you," then why was he not around to shield this child who could have done no wrong in the world? And if all things happen according to Him, then what was the purpose of this child's untimely death before his life was even able to start? And what's more, where was God when other Negroes were being sold like cattle and separated from their families? God ain't here, he thought. Maybe in the old Bible days, but he ain't here no more.

When he returned to the tipi, the lovely crimson finish of a bow made of bison horn seized his attention. He picked it up, pulled back, and released the deer-tendon drawstring. The strong snap shot the memory through his mind of the arrow that grazed him when they fought the Kaw. His left arm was still tightly bandaged, and he thought that he much rather preferred being shot over taking a direct hit from an arrow any day.

His fingers were shriveled-up prunes, and he rubbed them together and felt nothing, as if he were not actually touching himself. He rotated them over a smoldering fire until some feeling began to come back to them. Another beautiful blanket was laid out on the floor. He pulled it toward him, wrapped himself in it, and lay near the hot ashes for the night, while the horrid image of the dead child burned in his mind.

When he woke, the pink lights of the day were visible on the horizon. His strength was restored, and his ankle even began to decrease in swelling, though he still favored it as he walked uphill. He came to another peak and was eager to chart his course for the day, but again he was met with even more countless trees and hills in each direction.

His spirit became as heavy as the five-foot-tall stone that he now reclined on. He closed his eyes in defeat and stared up at the sky. A small sting of coldness began to touch his face. When he opened his eyes, hundreds of small white specs effortlessly floated down toward him.

"Great," he said to himself.

The snow silenced everything in the valley beneath him. His new clothes gave him relief from the chilly air. He took in the beauty of the landscape for another ten minutes before he continued to the west, hoping that he could find the same trail they had used to get to the Crow village and from there head south back to the Platte.

He covered eight miles that day, but as the last pink lights vanished from the sky, his view was still dominated by the endless horde of trees and the same was true the day after. Unbeknownst to the boy, the Crow braves had not given up finding him and were aided by his carelessness. He believed they would have given up by now and did not cover his tracks nor scatter his night camps.

The blistering pain and frigid temperatures continued to

torment his body. His only escape was his thoughts. The dead child that he had buried had planted himself in the boy's mind. Maybe that was why the Natives were called savages. Only a savage could perform an act such as that, right? No, he thought. There were whites who turned a blind eye to their own atrocities. Why were they not called savages?

His thoughts turned to the demonization of his own people and the treatment they endured while on this land that was, itself, savage. Every literature that he read described Africa as a "dark continent overrun with savages who, other than a loincloth, ran around as animals" and now he doubted every assertion about the continent and its people.

Perhaps this wasn't God's fault. What if God stayed out of the affairs of man, and it was man who allowed that child to be killed? It was man who allowed children to be sold like cattle.

He wasn't sure on this, but he smiled at those thoughts and commented on his growth in that area when the sharp point of an arrow pierced his left thigh and discharged a pain that shot through his entire body. He dropped to the ground, stiff as a log. Another arrow impaled the left side of his torso and caused his body to jerk as if he had been struck by lightning. His thin, lifeless body remained in place and would not move again.

The young brave with the long scar over his eye looked satisfied as he slowly stepped from behind a tree with his bow still flexed under the pressure of the pulled string. He relaxed the tension in the bow as he came closer and stood over the boy. With a hideous face, he examined his body. He seemed unsure of his next course of action, having never scalped a black before. He unsheathed his knife and reached for the thick puff of messy hair. The boy gripped the hatchet even tighter and turned over and plunged it deep into the left side of the brave's neck. The

Crow's body fell over and snagged the arrow that was still in the boy's thigh. The arrow moved inside of the wound, causing the boy to almost pass out from the pain.

The boy pushed the Crow off of him and watched blood erupt from his neck as his body shook and convulsed violently. The hatchet hadn't broken the Crow's neck, but he more than likely wished that it had. The boy was not much older than the Crow, and when he went to dislodge the hatchet from his neck, he stared at him. A strange understanding connected the two boys. The brave's eyes begged for the boy to kill him, and this the boy did, with several more hacks from the hatchet. He grabbed the Crow's robe and wiped at the blood that dripped from his arms, legs, and hands.

Before he could begin to feel anything about the mutilation, another arrow whizzed by his head. He immediately jumped up and began to limp away. Behind him, he heard large footsteps pounding against the ground as well as the breaking of twigs and branches and, of course, that terrible war whoop. He saw an opening from the trees and made his way as fast as he could toward it. By the time he saw that it was a cliff, he had gone too far to stop. He tumbled about fifteen feet, causing more damage to his already swollen ankle and the two arrow shafts that still stuck from his body. Pulsing adrenaline helped him ignore the pain, and he managed to stand and place his back to the rocky cliff where he stood still.

A few seconds later, a Crow in full war paint peered out above him with a bow in hand. From directly above the boy, her menacing face scanned the entire area like a machine, surveying the forestry on the opposite side of a small creek that led into a pond. She pulled back her bowstring and flung an arrow at a noise that turned out to be a squirrel. She spoke in his language to three men that were with her. The boy held his breath for what seemed to be an eternity. His lungs thumped and begged for air. He covered his mouth with his bloody right hand and quietly let air in and out of his body. After a minute of searching, the Crow moved on and continued to search north of the area.

The boy looked up and stepped away from the rock with uncertainty in each step. He turned around and now faced the huge boulders that made up the cliff. He dropped his gaze to the ground, and his heart dropped even further. Through a mass of twigs and branches that covered a crevice made from the cliffs, two soulless black eyes stared at him. They were surrounded by a large, agitated black face. The branches separated and the monster yawned, showing a set of razor-sharp teeth.

13

What Remains

Weeks earlier, the boy had stood in the shadow of a grizzly that dwarfed the black bear that now stared at him. He was sure that now no lesser bear could ever faze him, but the bear was still a bear. It did not take too kindly to being woken up while in its den. A low, pulsing sound came from deep in the beast's throat. It stood and began to crawl toward the boy on short, pointy claws that could easily rip into a man's flesh. The bear was a shell of its former self, having lost most of its mass while hibernating, but was, nevertheless, still dangerous. The boy slowly took a step in retreat. The pressure on his thigh reminded him of the broken arrow that still poked out of it. He winced as each step felt like a new arrow being shot into his leg, again and again.

"It's okay," he whispered. "I'm not gonna hurt you. You're a beautiful, nice bear." His words gently rolled out of his mouth, as soft as they would to a child.

The sweet nothings did nothing to appease the animal, and it continued to growl and move toward him. The boy reached to his waist and unsheathed a long hunting knife. He crouched while continuing to back away from the bear. Each time the boy took a step, the bear appeared to grow more emboldened and crawled forward.

As if it had a change of heart, the creature backed away. The momentary relief disappeared when the bear leaped toward him. It managed to find its claw on the boy's left side, right above the arrow. At the same time, the boy took a stab of his own just below the bear's neck. The knife struggled to pierce the thick muscle. Now fully committed to the attack, the bear charged the boy and knocked him to the ground. The boy threw up his left forearm in protection. The pulverizing force of the bear's bite nearly broke the bone in half. With his free right hand, the boy repeatedly bayoneted the same spot in the bear's neck until it lightened up its bite. What sounded like the screams of a wounded elderly man echoed throughout the area. A horrible, high-pitched yell that turned the boy's skin pale. He sat up on his butt, propped up on his elbows, as he watched the animal slither back to the thicket in which he had found it.

He gripped the bloody knife in his right hand and waited for the bear to emerge again. When it did not, he gave a sigh of relief and regained his composure. He braced his left arm on the ground to help him stand, and only now did he feel the full force of his newest injury. His entire body howled at him. He hobbled through the monotonous pine trees until he came to one and sat with his back against it.

This was the most pain he had ever felt, and he fully believed that nothing could ever be worse. His left hand was practically useless, and with his right, he grabbed a hold of the arrow in his thigh and began to pull it out. He stopped when he thought about Carl and how much blood he lost after the hatchet was removed. If he didn't find help soon, he knew he would die right there, alone in the woods, never to hear or see his loved ones again.

"I gotta see them again," he said to himself. "Even if I die at the door, I gotta." He took shelter under some brush and cried himself to sleep, wishing his mother were there to hold him. Each night becoming worse than the one prior.

The next day, he sat in front of a small fire pit with his legs out in front of him. His thigh was now double its normal size. The skin around the arrow shaft turned a dark-urine color. The terrible smell began to make him feel sick. To his left sat a curved powder horn, a stick with brush tied on the end of it, a small carpet made of bundled tree moss, and a pile of sage.

He used the sage to fuel his fire and grabbed the arrow shaft with his right hand. He was able to wiggle the shaft around, which meant that the arrow had not lodged itself in his bone. He hesitated to pull out the arrow and cried out to God. He wondered how Roy would have handled this situation and took three deep breaths. He counted, one, two, and yanked the remainder of the arrow out. The point of it ripped out some of the muscle it had lodged itself into. He tossed it into the trees, flinging blood everywhere. More of the thick, dark-red liquid started to emerge from the wound that needed to be closed up soon. He repeated the process with the arrow in his side, and this time was better prepared for the pain.

He used the buckskin shirt to soak up the blood from his thigh wound. The tip of the arrow left a deep, disgusting gash in his skin. He grabbed the powder horn and tapped small amounts of the gunpowder into the wound. His face erupted into a scowl when the saltpeter in the powder began to burn inside of the wound. He took his handmade moss carpet and placed it over the wound to protect himself from powder burn. He grabbed the stick and placed it over the fire. Once the brush caught the blaze, he cautiously swung it over to his thigh and breathed deeply.

His entire body began to tense up. The veins in his neck projected out as he began to curse at himself to gain confidence. Again, he thought about Roy and immediately set the lit brush against the wound. A small scorching fireball erupted on his thigh and fizzled out in two seconds. A tiny white cloud of smoke floated away in the wind, but the pain remained. He shook uncontrollably, exhaled, and cursed. It was ironic that this pain was worse than the actual shot itself. He looked at the melted gunpowder, ran his hand over it, and saw that the wound had stopped bleeding altogether.

Before admiring his work, he lay on his side and dropped the stinging gunpowder into the wound. Eager to get it over with, he wasted no time and set the powder on fire. It sizzled like water in a hot pan, and the burning sensation felt much worse than the wound on his thigh.

When he woke up, the sun was setting and half an inch of snow sat on his chest and thighs. Half frozen, he went about rebuilding the fire and spent another uncomfortable night in the forest.

His wounds had already become infected. The next morning, his leg and side were a greenish color. The pain was so great and constant that he had gotten used to it by now. Lying under a blanket of cloth and snow, he searched his hand around the crumbs in his knapsack. His stomach performed a cartwheel, and his head spun from all the blood he had lost. Laid out on the ground, he could not tell whether he was upside down or not, and he felt as if he were tumbling around. When he stabilized, he looked up at a gray sky, closed his eyes, and spoke out to whomever may have been listening.

"I could use a little help," he whispered out. "You've done more for less. Please, I just wanna get home, please."

He immediately thought of the burning bush and Jonah being swallowed by a whale. When he opened his eyes, he half expected a giant eagle to swoop down and pick him up. He would sit on its back while it brought him closer to the sun for warmth. It would carry him over the Crow and the Kaw, past the endless prairies, and down the mighty Missouri, all the way home.

Or perhaps he expected to hear the rushing of some undiscovered river that cut a straight path from where he was now back to Tennessee. And at the river a canoe would sit, waiting for him with furs and food already loaded, ready for its destined passenger. He had hoped and prayed for these things, but he remained lying on the ground. An occasional snowflake landed and then disappeared on his trembling face.

"You really don't work that way, huh?" he said, and he began to force himself to stand.

He now began to fear that he would have to amputate his leg from the thigh down in order to save the rest of his body. He envisioned swinging the hatchet down on his thigh. He could cut off an ankle or a foot, but not a thigh. He began to drag himself around the forest.

He was not quite sure of his direction, and at times he fell to the ground and would black out for an undetermined amount of time. When he would rise, he would return to the task of seeing his parents again. With large tears in his eyes, he would continue to creep and speak in an unintelligible gibberish. He pleaded with God to let him see the very people he had taken for granted, one last time.

He could hear his mother's laughter, a loud, colorful cackle that always seemed to pierce his ears more on Saturday mornings. He could hear his father scold him for his carelessness, selfishness, or a combination of the two. His heart yearned for one more of the lectures that he had despised so much. He lost track of days and how far he had walked. On swollen feet and ankles, he trudged around and swore death personified stared at him from behind a tree. The figure was tall, gaunt, and faceless. He called out to it, welcoming Death's sweet kiss. After being ignored, he screamed out to the Crow and mocked them, praying that anyone would find him.

On his ninth day in the forest, he was half blinded by hunger and fatigue. The branches scratched and ripped the scabs from his already calloused skin. He rejoiced when he came to a clearing. A small creek slowly ran in front of him, and he bent down to drink from it, looking more beast than man. His body failed him, and he fell once more and would not rise again on his own power. Now he realized and accepted that he would die in this place, another name added to a list of forgotten men.

He had asked to be free and to find adventure, and this was the result. His body remained stiff and motionless, but a redeeming thought drifted through his mind. This was what he had asked for, and as a man, he had to deal with the consequences. A faint smirk shot across his face.

But what'll happen to my soul? he wondered. His chest and stomach rose and fell with slow, deep breaths that signaled what was soon to come. His eyes were wide open, but he could not see anything nor could he make sense of the indistinct sounds that bounced around his ears. He mouthed the words "I'm sorry," before closing his eyes.

Two hunters, one black and one white, could not believe what stumbled out of the forest. At first they took him to be the Wendigo they had heard so much about and were frozen in terror. They ran toward him when they realized he was indeed human, though from the looks of him, not by much. Dirt and twigs were lodged in his mess of a hairstyle. His brown pupils appeared jet black and sat several inches back in their sockets, surrounded by a sea of red. Dried blood was caked over various wounds all around his body. With a rifle leveled at him, the man walked slowly toward the boy.

"Good God almighty. Ho! Jim, come take a gander at this."

The black man's name Murphy. He called his counterpart closer. They both picked up the boy and rested his arms over their shoulders. They listened to the faint breaths. They laid him over Murphy's horse, picked up their traps, and quickly escorted him back to their camp.

Three days later, he came to. He stared at the inside of a dark-yellow tent. For a while, he did not move, nor did he think. His mind remained blank as throbbing pain circulated throughout his entire body. When he finally went to sit up, the wound on his side reminded him of its presence, and he fell over to the ground and grabbed at it. He looked at his swollen thigh and ankle. His hand touched his face, and he felt the permanent scar that he received in New Orleans.

What the hell happened? Where am I? he asked himself.

His thigh, along with his midsection, forearm, and several other areas, were all tightly bandaged. With wide, innocent eyes of disbelief, he looked around at the tent and called out to his parents. Outside, men chattered indistinctly. A pair of moccasins and some colorful leggings sat in front of him. Still dazed and confused, he toiled to put them on. He stood up, and hobbled out of the tent.

Having not seen light for several days, he squinted at the setting sun. Like a once-thought-dead being from biblical reckoning, he emerged from the tent and began to remove his bandages. Around him, a group of men were busy going about their typical sundown camp rituals. When his eyes adjusted, he stared through bright, wide portals that looked mystified as he searched for his father and mother.

Gruff-looking men that he had never seen before were now watching him. Filthy, thin, and bearded, they were the most unappealing pack of men he had ever seen. Each was no more than five feet from a weapon, and they looked more than willing to use them. His heart raced as their eyes met his, and he stood in complete terror of what he had gotten himself into. Murphy had been driving a stake into the ground when he saw the boy exit the tent. He called out and walked over to him.

"Easy, easy," he said as he led him back to the tent and laid him down.

"Where am I? Who are you?" said the boy.

When Murphy looked at him, he looked into the eyes of an innocent child, much different than the eyes he had seen when they first discovered the boy.

"Hell if I know. We not too far from the Black Hills, where we found you. I'm Murphy, Murphy Young."

He helped the boy to lie back down. The flap of the tent opened, and an old man entered. He did not seem to pay much attention to the boy or Murphy. He squinted around the tent for something before leaving without saying a word.

"That's Mister Ross Sibble. He's the leader of this here company."

When Ross returned, he had a small stool in his hand. He placed it on the ground and sat down a few feet from the boy, who watched him with those large, pure eyes. He removed his hat and ran his hand through dull gray hair that was the same hue as his lengthy beard. He exchanged greetings with the boy and cleared his throat.

"Murphy here tells me that they stumbled on you half dead in the Black Hills?"

"What he says is as good as a guess as mine."

"So you don't recall how you came to be?"

"No, sir."

"Clearly it has to do with them Indins. Probably worked some of that Indin magic on him, Murphy. I told you."

Murphy made a face of disbelief but kept his mouth shut. Ross continued.

"Where are you from?"

"Tennessee," he said, surprised that he remembered it.

"Whose company were you with?"

"Company?"

"Yes, damnit. Ain't no Negro out here on his own accord, especially not as young as yourself. Fur trade? Captured by Indins?"

"I don't remember." Much like a child, he shuddered at the man's irritation.

"What is the last thing you recall?" Ross's face was now growing faint red with frustration.

"I was with my Paw goin' into Memphis. It was late summer, but I can't recall nothin' after that."

"Late summer! Poor child," Murphy said. "It's spring now!"

Ross turned to him as if he expected him to elaborate on some subliminal "Negro talk" that he was unaware of.

"Boss, he clearly came out here with some fur outfit. I make it that they all gone now, hence the arrow wounds we found in him, and he survived by runnin' in them Black Hills. Whatever he suffered, his brain couldn't catch a hold of it and just chucked it out, hence his memory bein' gone."

"But which outfit?"

"We won't know until we make it to the rendezvous and see who ain't there."

"Damn it, Murphy, if you wasn't a Negro, I'd say you was brighter than me. Sounds about right?" he said, looking to the boy.

"I don't know. I just want to go home."

"You're in luck. I'm sendin' some men, including Murphy here, back to St. Louis for more supplies. You can return with them."

"Thank you," the boy said, with a tear in his eye.

He spent his time idling around the camp, meeting the various men. They hailed him as some sort of a celebrity and all were eager to shake his hand and share their names with him. At night, the men gathered around him like children and would listen to him as he spoke in his sleep. He told of Indian parties more numerous than the buffalo and of scalpings, four- and two-legged beasts, killings and winter storms that would have vexed even the mighty polar bear. He cried of hardships and pain. His legend grew as men began to tell his story to others who in turn would tell it to other men in a grossly distorted way.

The day before their departure for St. Louis, he and Murphy had been fetching water from the river. The water was up to his knees and soothed the swelling he still had. He paused for a moment and surveyed the grassy countryside and endless hills. The sun glimmered off the crystal-clear water. He took in a deep breath of the fresh air and even managed to smile.

To the north, a detachment of men came over a hill toward the camp. As their features became visible, he dropped the pot. A group of Native people, led by two Americans, came to the camp.

"They don't mean no harm. They just here to trade. Them Crow are friendly to us," Murphy said. But the boy stood still with his mouth wide open with a shocked look on his face. Painful, unwanted memories began to flood back inside his mind.

The wide-eyed, innocent look that he had regained was now replaced with a dull nonchalance. Before, he had appeared new to this world and took in his surroundings with a childlike curiosity. He overturned stones and took notice of the insects under them. He would stare off at the hills in the distance, imagining what was out there.

But now, his eyes held a strong pessimism, as if his mind was convinced about what he and the world truly were. The faint smile he recovered gave way to a bleak, unimpressed expression.

Out in front of the Crow was Cut Belly. He surveyed the camp and when he locked eyes with the boy, he shot him a devilish smirk. Cut Belly looked back at the female brave who had nearly killed the boy. She looked over at him as well and shot the same smirk as they went farther into camp to commence their trade, which continued well into the night.

One of the items that the Crow brought was the boy's old knapsack. They claimed that the Blackfeet were responsible for attacking a party of Americans and that they had come upon it and other items after surprising the Blackfeet in camp.

"Murphy," the boy cried out. He spied the item from afar. "What's that?"

"You see that knapsack?"

"Yeah, what of it?"

"Can you trade for it?"

"The hell you want that for? You don't wanna take the personal belongings of a dead man. Ain't nothin' good ever came from it."

"It's mine."

"Yours? I thought you didn't know how you came to be."

"Keep your voice down. All my memories came back after I seen him."

He looked up at Cut Belly, who seemed to pay him no attention.

"What?"

"I came out here with a fur company. General Zebulon's outfit. Cut Belly and his men slaughtered the entire company. Only four of us survived, and they made us run naked through the forest to escape. I'm the only one that made it out."

"Good God," Murphy said.

"That's my bag, and I'll do anything in the world to get it back. Please, Murphy, help me out. I don't have nothin' to give you for it, but please out of your heart, help me. My papers are in the bag."

"Papers? Freedom papers?"

"Yes, sir."

This evoked some sort of emotion in Murphy, who himself was a runaway. He spoke to Ross Sibble, and after much convincing, the knapsack along with some of Roy's belongings were in the boy's possession. He pulled out the beat-up tin and extracted the papers. He embraced them and at the same time placed Roy's bear-tooth necklace on him. For just a moment, all seemed right with the world.

187

The next day, he set out with the group on their way back to St. Louis. They rode horseback until they reached the Missouri River, where they built a large boat on which to finish the final leg of their journey. In their night camps, the boy lay silent. He twirled his tin of papers in his hand and half listened as the men spoke of their longings for home, family, and most of all, their favorite whores in St. Louis.

The boy was in a constant whirlwind of emotions. Every now and then, tears flowed from his lifeless eyes. They were large tears of the joy at him miraculously still being alive. Only after nearly having the gift taken from him did he begin to appreciate the importance of it. Perhaps God kept him alive for a special purpose, he thought. But then the haunting image of the child's mangled body in the tipi tossed it aside and dropped him into another bout of depression.

More importantly, what would he say to his parents? And they to him? He was afraid to explain to them what he had been through. How would they react to their beloved child now being a seasoned killer? He thought about how he couldn't go home but quickly rejected the idea, understanding that if he couldn't go and speak to his parents, then he could truly go to no one in this world.

He thought solely about his father. The man was well respected, hardworking, and intelligent, with a loving family. Sure, he wasn't some brave adventurer who killed two black bears with his hands. He wasn't some General who was known for his heroism on the battlefield. He wasn't even some man who indiscriminately smacked racists on the daily, but that didn't make him any less of a man. Perhaps following in his father's footsteps, in the boy's own way, wouldn't be so bad.

Two months from their departure, he found himself back

in the lush green forests of Tennessee. He passed through Memphis, which had grown much in the past year. A wanted poster with his portrait and description on it sat plastered on the outside wall of a general store. He stood in front of the poster and stared at the sweet face of an innocent child. He had not seen that face in almost a year, nor would he ever see it again. In fact, the drawing on the poster looked to be a different person altogether.

A filthy man dressed in rags watched this from afar. He slithered over toward the boy. Without a doubt, he intended to ask the boy for his pass. He opened his mouth.

"Let me . . ." He cut his speech short.

The boy's sharp gaze pierced the man's soul, causing him to drop the matter entirely as he went on about his day. The boy pulled the poster off the wall. He folded it and placed it in his knapsack. He traded some of the handmade jewelry and weapons he had acquired for an old mule that looked like it could barely walk under its own weight. He carefully jumped onto the animal, and they limped on toward the east.

It was late afternoon of the next day when he came within view of his wooden home. Sweat overflowed from his pores, soaking his entire body and even the defeated moccasins that he still wore. The mule cried tears of joy when the boy got off. His home sat quiet and simple with the hot sun retreating behind it. He limped up to the door and gave it a light tap, so light that not even he could hear it over the sounds of the chickens out back.

He still had not thought about what to say to his mother. How could he face her after all that he had done? She would shun him and claim that the devil got a hold of him. With a heavy heart that itself reached out for the door, he made up his mind to head back out toward the west. His soul had been lost there, and he would go to find it, never to be seen again. He struggled to pull his feet away from the porch, and soon he was on the road again with a face wet with tears.

He was a quarter of a mile down the road before he turned the mule back. He jumped off it and hobbled to the door. With all the strength he could muster, his right hand pounded on the door with thunderous impact. The next ten seconds felt like an eternity. When the door opened, he stared into his mother's eyes. He witnessed them shift from cold and uninviting to the warm pools of brown that they had been a year prior. Dark bags sat under them, and slivers of gray were now in her hair. She nearly fainted and grabbed a hold of the door for support.

"David?" she said. "Is that you?"

The boy's hair was a tangled mess and nearly a foot long when stretched. The childish look of innocence on his face had been left in New Orleans nearly a year prior, and now small patches of facial hair sat on his once-unstained face. She stared at the scar on his cheek, the torn moccasins on his feet, and the bandaged left arm that he would never have full feeling or control over again. She focused on it and gasped.

His eyes were tired and told of his many misfortunes. She grabbed him by the sweat-soaked buckskin shirt and pulled him down to her, realizing that he had grown taller, broader in the time she had not seen him. Inside, his father sat at a table that gave a view of the front door. A single tear escaped from his eye. He had never seen the man run until today. The large man almost knocked the boy and his mother over as he enveloped them with his massive arms. His sister appeared next, followed by his younger brothers, who had both grown like weeds since the last time he had seen them.

"I'm so sorry," he said, before he burst out into tears and pulled them all closer to him than they had ever been before.

Epilogue

Nine months later, a letter arrived at a small home in Tennessee. The boy's mother tiptoed to his room and found him in bed. Her small, delicate hand violently shook him awake, and she dropped a letter onto his chest. His name was beautifully written in cursive on a lovely purple envelope that smelled of lilac. The boy rubbed his stale eyes and sat up to stretch. He then opened the letter and read aloud.

"Dear Mister Freeman,

I was unsure of where to address it, so I am hoping that this letter will find you in good health. Our last encounter proved to be very unfortunate, indeed, but I am proud to present you with an opportunity of a lifetime. This very moment, the British are losing their stronghold on the Oregon Territory. This quite lovely tract of land will soon be available for American settlement, and I am extending you the chance to run ahead of the competition. I offer you employment with the New Frontier Fur Company, as this region is abounded with many fur-bearing animals. Upon trapping and amassing a small fortune, we shall purchase land and sell tracts of it to future settlers. I am most excited for this venture and look forward to your joining me in this enterprise. I can be reached at following address and eagerly await your response.

Sincerely,

Sir Colin Temecula. P.S. G.A.Z."

There was silence throughout the room. Disbelief painted the boy's face.

"One of your friends?" his mother said.

"Somethin' like that."

Glossary

Breechcloth – A long piece of animal skin used to cover the privates

Buckskin – The preserved hide of a deer; typically used for clothing

Coon – This sense of the word was used by early mountain men as an affectionate term to each other

Cracker – Derogatory term for white people

Fur trade – Worldwide industry that, at its peak in the 1800s, consisted of using the fur from North American beavers to make hats that were worn as a status symbol in Europe. Men traveled from all around the world to trap the animals and hoped to get rich by selling the fur. As a result of over-trapping, beavers became less common and the fur trade increasingly moved westward until fashion trends changed in the 1840s, rendering the fur of the animal useless.

Half-breed – Derogatory term often used to describe someone born of a European father and a Native mother

Hoss – Affectionate term used by the mountain men when

referring to one another

Indin - Shortened form of the word Indian

Injun - Casual corruption of the word Indian

Jakes - An outdoor toilet without any plumbing; an outhouse

Leggings - Often made of deer skin, they are used to protect the wearer's legs. Can be thought of as tube-like footless pants for some Native tribes.

Moccasins - Shoes often made of deerskin; often worn by mountain men who obtained them from trading with Native people; also called "mocs"

Nigger - Offensive ethnic slur directed at black people

Queer - Strange; peculiar

'Ree - Shortened form of Arikara, a tribe of Native people especially known for their conflicts with early mountain men

Savages - Derogatory term used here to refer to Native people

Scalp - A common practice of the time; to cut off a piece of one's scalp and hair, often with a knife. Scalps were often used as trophies of war

Shianne - Corruption of the word Cheyenne; a tribe of Native people

Tipi - Tent-like structure usually made with animal skins. Used by SOME of the Native people that lived in the region of the Great Plains

Wagh - Exclamation used by mountain men to show surprise

Wendigo - A mythical creature believed by certain Native tribes to reside in forests and terrorize humans in the area

Discussion Guide

What drives the boy to run away from home? How do you think you would handle living under similar circumstances? What would you do?

What is your view on how the Native people had been treated? Are their reactions justifiable?

Which character did you identify most with? Why? How did this character change throughout the story? What this character have to realize about himself or herself to change?

Why do you think Roy took the boy under his wing? Who are the mentors in your life? How did you feel when Old Roy died?

Was the author descriptive with the settings and people? Were you able to visualize yourself in these places? Did you have a good picture of what the characters looked like?

What were the major themes and are they relevant in your life? How so?

Did the author convey the era and setting of the story well? Did it come across as authentic? Is this a time period you would want to live in? Why or why not?

Did this book hook you immediately or did it take some time to get into?

If Carl had not shown the Crow the stolen belongings, how do you think the book would have ended? Would the group have lived or would the General's carelessness have gotten them killed, anyway?

If this book were to be made into a movie, whom would you cast for the different roles?

What do you think was the main message that the author was attempting to get across?

Do you know anyone who is similar to the characters? If so, how?

Think of the General's tragic backstory and his personality as an adult. Everyone has a story and a past that makes them how they currently are. Has this story changed your opinion about anyone in your life?

The novel takes place in the early 1800s. How did the use of certain slurs and terms make you feel? How would you handle those words being said to, or around you?

After reading the epilogue, what do you think the boy will do? Has he learned his lesson or do you think his experiences have changed him too much?

About the Author

A native of Detroit, Michigan, D'Andre Walker went on to Michigan State University where he received his bachelor's degree in civil engineering. When he's not constructing a highway or bridge, he is reading, writing or training for his next amateur boxing tournament. Based in Detroit, he is currently living in Central California, working on his next project. He can be reached at fwoodwardpublishing@gmail.com

You can connect with me on:

■ https://www.facebook.com/DreWalkTheAuthor

∂ https://www.instagram.com/walkman93_

Made in the USA
Coppell, TX
08 December 2019

12575992R00120